"We're truly s ~~looking for us~~

"If they got the helicopter's signal, if they heard the pilot's SOS, yes, someone will come looking. Eventually, when the weather clears. By all indications, there's going to be snow between here and base camp within the next day or two. Chances are good that the weather is keeping anyone from looking for us. We can't sit here and wait for that. We'll end up dead. We're going to rest for the night, as dark's falling soon. At dawn we begin our walk out."

"How are you going to know which way to go? How do I know you really know what you're doing, that you're not taking us to our deaths?"

Daniel stared at Cassie, who'd come to mean more to him than people he'd known for months, years in some cases. In only a matter of—he checked his fitness band for the time—eight hours. "You don't. You're right—I could be making it all up. As I see it, there isn't much choice here, is there?"

Former naval intelligence officer and US Naval Academy graduate **Geri Krotow** draws inspiration from the global situations she's experienced. Geri loves to hear from her readers. You can email her via her website and blog, gerikrotow.com.

Stranded in the Mountains

GERI KROTOW

LOVE INSPIRED
INSPIRATIONAL ROMANCE

LOVE INSPIRED®
INSPIRATIONAL ROMANCE

Recycling programs
for this product may
not exist in your area.

ISBN-13: 978-1-335-42706-9

Stranded in the Mountains

Copyright © 2022 by Geri Krotow

For questions and comments about the quality of this book, please contact us
at CustomerService@Harlequin.com.

Love Inspired
22 Adelaide St. West, 41st Floor
Toronto, Ontario M5H 4E3, Canada
www.LoveInspired.com

Printed in U.S.A.

There shall no evil befall thee, neither shall any plague come nigh thy dwelling. For he shall give his angels charge over thee, to keep thee in all thy ways.
—*Psalm* 91:10–11

To Steve, Alex and Ellen

Chapter One

"I'm here for the flight to Saglak Bay." Cassie Edmunds dumped her heavy backpack and duffel bag on the floor next to a tiny service counter in the small Canadian airplane hangar. As she spoke to the only other person in sight, the middle-aged woman behind the tall desk, she eyed the few aircraft on the strip outside the weathered building and tried to keep her stomach from flipping. Nain, Labrador, made Hershey, Pennsylvania, feel like it was a world away.

Her head was spinning after nearly twenty-four hours of travel, mostly in planes smaller than she'd prefer. She'd flown from Harrisburg, to Toronto, to Goose Bay, then to this tiny outpost in the northernmost part of the province. Cassie wasn't enthralled with flight in any form. She preferred both feet on the ground, preferably in her favorite patent leather Italian loafers instead of these clunkier, albeit practical, hiking boots she wore. She was willing to do anything for her grandmother, however, and was grateful that at least she didn't have to rocket to the moon. But going so far away from home and so much closer to the Arctic certainly felt like space travel.

She wiggled her toes in the brand-new waterproof purple-and-gray hiking boots she'd found on sale back home. At least she'd be able to keep up with the guide that was taking her tourist group into the deeper, lesser visited parts of Torngat Mountains National Park. She'd sent up countless prayers that against all odds she'd find out where her great-grandmother had crashed a B-17 bomber during World War II. Great-granny Eugenia had been ferrying the plane as part of the Women Airforce Service Pilots (WASP) program. All male pilots were sent to the war front, but more flyers were needed to get the planes from production factories to the bases both at home and overseas. Great-Granny Eugenia had been one of the many women who'd stepped up and served the country as pilots. Cassie had never met Eugenia, yet her respect for the woman gave her strength to commit to this long trip.

Cassie's Grandma Rose, Eugenia's daughter, waited back in Hershey for the results of this trip. Yes, Cassie hated flying in small aircraft, but not fulfilling her octogenarian grandma's wish wasn't an option.

"Found it! You're on the flight manifest." The woman's reply brought Cassie back to the present, her kind eyes peering at her monitor. She gave Cassie a wide smile. "Welcome to Nain, then. You're with Sean—he'll be taking you along with the other passenger as soon as he returns from his last flight. We're also waiting for the second passenger to check in." Her fingers moved quickly over a keyboard. "His flight from Goose Bay is delayed."

"I thought I was the only passenger. I've chartered a private flight." And paid dearly for it, with most of her savings. Not that Cassie had any regrets about the cost. This trip would satisfy both her, and Grandma Rose's, curiosity about their family.

Grandma Rose wanted to know for certain where her mother had perished during World War II, back when Rose was just a tiny tot. The family had received Eugenia's dog tags and an approximate location for where the plane went down, sent to the war office by an anonymous witness in Canada, but it was in the 1940s, in the middle of the fighting, and her remains were never recovered. The incredibly remote location of the crash didn't help, especially in the era before GPS. An exact location for the plane was never communicated, and the impossible conditions that plagued the geographic area for eight of twelve months per year had made it infeasible for Cassie's family to search for Eugenia's remains before now. Even the governments of both nations had deemed Eugenia, and her crew, as lost during the war effort.

When Cassie read about the possibility that several different World War II planes, including three B-17s, had recently been rediscovered by Inuit locals, she began to plan her trip. Cassie had always been fascinated by her family tree, which morphed into becoming an avid genealogist as an adult. This last couple of years she'd managed to fill in the blank spots for many relatives, going back to almost medieval times. But she didn't have much of anything on Eugenia, who had died before she'd been of an age to consider future generations and save family artifacts.

Cassie disliked blank spots, whether they were about historical facts or an unlabeled storage container, one of her organizing pet peeves.

She knew it was a slim chance she'd see the actual aircraft her great-grandmother had piloted, but she'd be able to return home and let her family know that she'd paid respects for the entire family. And, deep down, she had faith that she just might glean more insight into Eugenia's last flight.

With that in mind, she wasn't about to allow a miscommunication to keep her from getting to the Torngat Mountains Base Camp on time, as planned.

Cassie pulled out her phone and pulled up the original airline ticket. She flashed a wide smile at the woman. "Here you go. I definitely paid for a private charter."

The attendant took her reading glasses off and gave Cassie a frank look. "We often need to adjust our schedule this time of year. As I'm sure you know, the park is only open for five weeks, and the demand is high. Sean's been flying nearly round-the-clock this past month, allowing for the crew rest required by law. Don't worry, honey. He'll get you there in no time once he's back."

Cassie bit her lower lip as she tried to maintain her go-to no-worries-here expression she presented to her business clients. A professional organizer by trade, Cassie struggled to keep her attitude positive when she wasn't helping a client re-do closets overflowing with unused, tag-still-on clothing, or a garage packed full of toys that their children had outgrown a decade earlier. At work, Cassie was in complete control. Out here in the world of remote travel? A prickly flush crept up her nape. She had zero control over the outcome of this trip, no matter what skill set she thought she possessed. If not for her faith, she'd have never left Pennsylvania.

"I understand, ma'am, and I appreciate your help. Is there a place I can wait, then?" She looked around the space, noting the decided lack of seating. Wi-Fi was probably a luxury, too.

"Yes, go through the double doors over there and you'll find a selection of vending machines." The woman looked at her watch. "If you hurry, you might catch the cook and get something from the café grill, too."

"Thank you. I'll be back in a bit." Cassie's stomach grumbled. Once through the doors she found other people walking around, also in search of a late lunch. To her dismay the tiny dining counter had a closed sign, but she was able to use her credit card to snag a coffee with milk, and a packaged muffin.

"Not much to choose from." A warm male voice wrapped around her as she waited for her coffee to brew and she turned to its source. A man stood next to her, his blue eyes pleasant. He was a solid foot taller than her and appeared to be close in age to her thirty years. His tan skin emphasized laugh lines at the corners of his eyes, and were those dimples? She couldn't stop herself from reciprocating his smile as she held up the crushed muffin.

"This is my lunch." She pulled the full paper coffee cup from the machine and immediately winced. "Whoa, this is hot!"

"Here." He took the cup from her and set it atop the

machine, easily reachable with his height. "I had to let mine cool a bit, too."

"Thank you." Gratitude swelled in her heart. In the middle of nowhere, kindness from an unknown person was a special blessing.

"Didn't you eat on the flights up here?"

She blinked. As nice as this guy was, she didn't want to admit to a complete stranger that she couldn't eat in-flight thanks to her motion sickness.

"I'm sorry—it's none of my business. Enjoy the rest of your trip." The stranger took her cup from atop the vending machine, handed it back to her, and turned to walk away.

"No, wait!" He turned back, looked at her. She took a step toward him. "It's not you. I get motion sick and by the last flight up here, I didn't want to risk eating anything." Her cheeks burned but something about being in the middle of nowhere allowed her to let go of her usual reticence. Working with unpredictable clients called on her to be in control, the calm note amid often chaotic family dynamics. Her patrons often juggled raising children, caring for aging parents and maintaining career demands. But she wasn't facing a stressed-out parent. She was looking into the kindest eyes she'd ever seen.

"I get it." Genuine compassion made his deep voice all the more soothing.

"You do? You get motion sick?" She had a hard time associating such an athletically built man with any kind of physical weakness. In Cassie's family health was everything. Since she was a young child, she remembered hearing Grandma tell her that "your health is everything." To admit she wasn't feeling well wasn't easy for her.

"Not so much anymore, as I've learned to manage it better, but sometimes it can creep up out of nowhere." He shrugged. "It's not a moral defect by any means." His bright smile chased her worry about the next and last leg of her trip north away. Her still queasy stomach reminded her that she'd come close to tossing her breakfast on the previous flight, but this man's upbeat approach soothed her nerves. Maybe she could make it without getting sick. Take some photos of the breathtaking scenery she'd seen on the internet.

"Thanks, I needed to hear that."

"Sure thing. By the way, I noticed you from Goose Bay, though. Mine just got in. We were running late."

Cassie opened her mouth to reply but the doors to the hangar burst open and a large man with a brown leather flight jacket held up a clipboard. "Edmunds! Sturges! Departing to Saglak Bay!" The pilot's deep voice boomed in the small space and she almost dropped her precious meal, coffee and all.

"I'm here!" She couldn't risk missing this flight.

"Sturges here." The man she'd been talking to answered in unison with her. Cassie looked at him, realization dawning.

"We're on the same flight to Torngat Mountains National Park?" This was the passenger she'd been thinking not-so-kind thoughts about only minutes earlier?

He nodded. "Appears so. I suggest you finish your meal now. This aircraft will be too small to enjoy it."

"Thanks for the heads-up." Her skin tightened across her face as she forced a smile. Cassie already knew it was going to be a helicopter and wasn't thrilled with the reminder. She walked ahead and checked in with the pilot, who introduced himself as Sean. He gave them both ten minutes to gather their belongings, use the restroom, and for Cassie, to eat. She sat atop her solidly packed duffle bag and tried to enjoy the stale blueberry muffin and cooling drink that in her opinion had zero relation to actual coffee. The man traveling with her walked up, set his much larger backpack down.

"I'm Daniel Sturges." He held out his hand.

"Cassie Edmunds." She tucked the last bite of muffin into her mouth, wiped her hand, and shook his. *Firm, strong, competent.* The adjectives ran through her mind unbidden.

"Nice to meet you, Cassie. Is it your first time visiting the Torngat Mountains?"

She nodded. "Yes, but I'm not going as a tourist. Not really. I'll be with a group but I'm not here for the polar bears or other wildlife." Why was she talking so fast? More importantly, what was it about Daniel that made her feel she needed to tell him everything? "I'm—I'm on a research trip of sorts." Friendly banter was one thing, but telling a complete stranger about Grandma Rose's big wish, and Great-grandma Eugenia's war tragedy, was something else.

Take a breath, say a prayer. She couldn't stop her smile at Grandma Rose's advice, always a comfort to her heart. Cassie took a quick moment to send up her heart thoughts to God.

Daniel was quiet for several minutes and she wondered if he'd noticed her eyes were closed, if he'd realized she was praying. Why did she care what he thought about it? She opened her eyes and caught him smiling at her.

"So tell me, Cassie. Are you on a historical type of tour, by any chance?"

"Kind of."

"How interesting." His immediate enthusiasm whisked away her concerns and suddenly she wished they were in the helicopter, where the engine noise would preclude conversation. Daniel's astute gaze gave her an unsettled feeling under her rib cage, made her question each and every word she spoke. And she'd only just met him. It wasn't as if he was the only nice guy she'd ever met. Daniel exuded the kind of confidence that she'd rarely experienced. It had to come from a deep sense of self, of knowing what mattered. Grandma had it. Quiet joy, and peace. No matter what else was going on, good or bad.

Or maybe jet lag was kicking in and she was overthinking everything. It was a hazard of her need for orderliness.

"Edmund, Sturges, let's go!" Sean the pilot stood a few feet away and didn't bother to look over his shoulder as he made for the exit to the runway.

Phew. Her chaotic thoughts about Daniel couldn't continue, with this last flight to focus on.

Keep telling yourself that.

"That's our signal." Daniel offered to help her with her small duffel and hiking backpack but she shook her head.

"I'm good." A sense of accomplishment swelled in her core. She'd taken particular care to pack as minimally as possible, so that she'd be able to manage her own luggage. After studying the tour company's website and consulting her hiking friends who'd gone on similar wilderness trips, she'd chosen a backpack with an attachable duffel bag. Cassie had everything she'd need for the next two weeks, including several protein options in case her hunger was greater than what the tour promised to provide.

Remember why you're here.

As much as she appreciated Daniel's friendliness, she wasn't about to concern herself with getting to know him any better. Not when her immediate focus had to be on not getting sick on this helicopter ride. After they landed, the tour would require her every thought, and lots of prayers.

She took her time leaving the hangar, purposefully trailing behind Daniel and their pilot. Cassie wanted the few minutes extra to regroup, to say a silent prayer of gratitude that she was about to see her dream come true. There wasn't any room to worry about a stranger's opinion of her, nor did she want to waste any energy in the wrong direction. She didn't know a whole lot about where she was going, save for her research, but one thing Cassie was certain of was that she was going to need all of her strength to get through the next two weeks.

"Hey, Sean, can I talk to you for a minute?" Daniel stood with the pilot on the tarmac, Cassie heading toward them from the hangar but still several yards away.

"Make it quick. We're fighting the weather everyday up here."

"Is there any way you can fly over the Nachvak Fjord on the way to Base Camp?"

"That's a bit out of the way for me, pal." Sean spoke with ease, probably used to personal requests on charters.

"Okay, I thought I'd ask. I'm hiking it with a guide over the next several weeks and it'd be worth seeing from the air first."

"Let me guess, you're going to be the one to find one of the planes?" Sean grunted.

"Maybe. One of the B-17s in particular."

"Buddy, many have tried. The news reports and the drone photos made it look like it's easy-peasy to get to the wrecks, but in fact they're still incredibly remote, even for up here. There's no direct way to them, and no time of year that is one-hundred percent safe to go. More power to you, though. Time and the weather here make searches more difficult than any of us would like. It's challenging to retrace any route, depending upon the weather. But a one-time, hiked-in path? Forget it."

"I'm only asking for an opportunity if it arises, Sean." He said a quick, silent prayer. *Please let Sean keep an open mind.*

Sean looked out at the horizon, which looked like a normal summer day this far north. Clear skies, mountains all around. "Tell you what, I'll see what I can do. But no promises."

"Thanks, man." Daniel shook Sean's hand and turned to help Cassie, who'd walked up. "Here, let me get those on board for you." He reached for her backpack, a smaller version of his, and single duffel.

"I'm fine, really." Her pretty face lit up with a smile

that made her blue eyes sparkle. He gave her points for stoicism but found it suddenly important that she enjoy the flight as much as he expected to.

"It's no problem." He took the bags after she let go. "It'll be a great adventure, trust me."

Daniel climbed aboard and stowed their bags, then waited for Cassie to get seated before taking the only other seat available, next to her. Sean took his seat and looked over his shoulder at them. "Get ready for the most beautiful flight of your lives, folks. First, let's review some safety features." Sean ran down a checklist and concluded by nodding at the bag Daniel had stowed his on top of. "That large yellow duffel has everything we'd ever need in the wilderness, just in case. But trust me, we'll be at base camp before you know it and you'll be off on your vacations." Sean turned to the front and began to flip switches, call into the small control tower.

Daniel looked through the small patch of cockpit window visible to him and hoped it'd be enough to keep his stomach still. He hadn't been lying to Cassie when he'd admitted he'd had his share of motion sickness. He was a high school history teacher for ten months of the year, driving a desk. But his summer vocation—he couldn't call his passion for treasure hunting anything less than a calling—necessitated ingenious travel that often put him in aircraft like this sporty helicopter. He'd learned to look at the horizon, do deep breathing, and appreciate the hawk's view from above the earth. And pray. Not all in that order.

His temporary traveling partner appeared to be his age and had a smile that would cause any man looking for a life partner to pause. Daniel wasn't in the market for a girlfriend, though, much less a big commitment. Ever since he'd broken up with the one woman he'd ever gotten serious enough with to ask to marry him, he'd kept it casual and noncommittal. He'd met his former fiancée right when he began his job several years ago. She'd taught French and they both had so much in common on paper it seemed a natural fit. But she'd not encouraged his treasure hunting trips, and in fact, had suggested he work hard to become a school administrator to ensure a higher paycheck for their future. Daniel certainly believed a father needed to provide for his family, but he knew God had blessed him with a gift for teaching. In the end, his desire to be in the classroom during the school year, and to be in the field during school breaks, proved to him that they were on different wavelengths. They split amicably. She ended up moving out of state and was happily settled with her husband and kids in the Philly area.

He dated here and there when back home in Pittsburgh, but kept it relaxed and more on a friend basis with the women he met. Maybe if he found a woman who understood why he needed to search for historical artifacts each summer, when most teachers enjoyed maximum family time, he'd change his mind. Until then, his social life wasn't a priority.

As the engine started above them he couldn't stop the roar of excitement pumping through his veins. This was going to be his biggest find to date, if he was successful in unearthing the aircraft that reportedly crashed in the most remote region of Newfoundland and Labrador, almost eighty years ago. He'd found several other crash sites over the past five years and intended this adventure to be no different. Daniel thrived on setting goals and accomplishing them.

Maybe too much, bud.

He ignored his conscience. True, it might seem greedy to an outsider to see how hard he worked each summer to earn an extra paycheck or two from the contractors who hired him to search for treasure, with sizable bonuses when found. Never mind that Daniel never signed a contract unless the employer guaranteed that any found treasure would be donated to a museum, or its appropriate national or indigenous source.

Any naysayers didn't know what Daniel did with his extra funds.

Once his basic necessities were covered, Daniel invested in something he'd promised himself he'd do long ago. He wanted to start his own business in historical trekking, to include extreme wilderness survival. A way to encourage high school youth to explore the outdoors while increasing their zeal for history. After this trip, if he found the B-17 and its treasure, he'd have enough for the down payment on the plot of thirty acres he'd had his eye on ever since it had been posted for sale last month. He'd scoured the real estate ads for years, dreaming of finding the perfect plot of land in Western Pennsylvania to launch his vision. When the parcel in the Laurel Mountains had become available, he'd been able to think of little else.

"Buckle in, folks. There are two fronts coming, one off the ocean and the other from out west. We're going to be rocking and rolling!" Sean shouted as he prepared to take off. Without warning, the helicopter lifted vertically up, up, up, the ground quickly fading below them.

Daniel gave him a thumbs-up but Sean was engrossed in flying, so he looked at Cassie, in the seat beside him. Her eyes were shut tight, her hands clasped in her lap, the white knuckles sticking out like pearls, matching the pallor of her skin. Without hesitation, he reached over and placed his hand on hers. He knew it was bold but he couldn't help but try to comfort her. He'd never forgotten his first helicopter flight, or how being so far from anything familiar had overwhelmed him the first time he'd trekked far from Pennsylvania. At first she didn't react and he gave her hand a soft squeeze, hoping she'd interpret it as a sign of reassurance. He was rewarded when her eyes opened and she peeked at him, as if risking her life to do so.

Would he be able to give her the comfort she needed? He might be a trained survival hiker but he had no idea how to fly a helicopter, no power over the weather Sean promised they were about to face. He could reassure her that he'd been through countless rough situations while in flight, that the time in the air, no matter how turbulent, would be worth it once she landed at Base Camp and beheld the most singularly pristine territory on the planet. But it was impossible to have a detailed conversation while the weather tossed them around like ping-pong balls in a dryer.

The helicopter dipped and rose like a roller coaster and he saw the sheer terror in Cassie's wide blue eyes. And wished he had some instant, calming words at the tip of his tongue.

You could pray.

He dismissed the errant thought. He believed in God and prayed often enough, but would it be inappropriate to ask a total stranger? Yes. Although if the flight grew any choppier, prayer with a woman he didn't know would be the least of his worries. If Sean had to make an emergency landing, they could all be stranded for days, weeks in this remote part of the world.

Another quick loss of altitude had his stomach flipping and jaw clenching. The tiny flicker of something he rarely acknowledged began to gain ground in his mind, adroitly clawing into his peace of mind.

Fear.

Chapter Two

❧

"Sit tight back there!" Sean's voice echoed over the audio system in their helmets. Daniel couldn't move, transfixed by Cassie's gaze, beseeching him to do something, anything, to make it all go away.

"It'll be okay!" he yelled slowly over the engine, with exaggerated enunciation. Cassie blinked, then nodded. Daniel had no idea why he struggled to muster the faith he usually found more readily, unless it was truly because he was afraid, too. And why wouldn't he be? It was never a guarantee that a flight would land safely.

Be with us, God. Thank You.

As soon as he offered up the private prayer, he felt better. Cassie seemed to have relaxed a bit, too. Maybe she'd said her own prayer.

After several more minutes, the flight leveled out. Daniel realized he wanted Cassie to enjoy her first trip to the Torngat Mountains and he knew if she wasn't willing to look out the window she'd miss so much. He decided to ignore the question the still, small voice kept pressing at him.

Why do you care so much about a total stranger?

"Cassie, trust me, it'll be easier for you if you keep your eyes open and look out the window. Turn your head—there, toward the mountains." He pointed at the window that arced away from her seat, and noticed she turned her head and focused her eyes on the distant view. The aircraft lurched forward, and they were catapulted against their restraints. This was the roughest start to a flight Daniel had ever experienced, but Sean had warned them. He did his best to keep a neutral expression in place. He didn't want to alarm Cassie.

Odd. He'd never worried about upsetting a virtual stranger, no matter how nice, before.

The noise level prevented further conversation, and Daniel fought down the urge to continue to "help" Cassie. She was a grown woman and had made a decision to go this far north; she'd get through this. He did wonder about her research that she'd mentioned, but reminded himself that he had enough to focus on with his project. And he needed the paycheck a successful mission would provide. Teaching was his true vocation but the public school salary made living in the Pittsburgh area tight. Taking contracts from wealthy investors to uncover historical treasure had become a solid source of extra income for him and his youth camp dreams. Plus, it often gave him great practical information to add to his American and World History syllabi.

A seasoned extreme weather hiker, he'd come prepared for the worst. The Torngat Mountains, and in fact the entire Newfoundland-Labrador northern region, were notorious for their horrible summer weather. He hoped for the best with the long days of summer sunshine to guide him in his search efforts, but prepared for the unexpected gales and even snow, depending upon elevation.

The helicopter soared upward on what he assumed was a gust of warm air, then it immediately dropped and shuddered as the weather took hold. Looking out his window, Daniel made out the Torngat Mountains through a tiny sliver of parted clouds. They were close; no more than another ten minutes to go. Sean was handling the flight controls well, and Daniel leaned forward to tell him that but was halted by the stony set to Sean's jaw, sweat covering his face. Daniel's stomach clenched. In all his travels, he'd never seen a pilot look so frightened. He shifted his gaze out in front of them, to what Sean was seeing that he wasn't.

Through the cockpit window the peaks had disappeared into a swirling, roiling mass of white-and-black mist. As soon as he realized he was looking at a deadly cloud bank, their view disappeared and the sound of countless rocks hitting the airframe echoed in the cabin. *Hail.*

A hand gripped his forearm and he looked at it, uncomprehending. *Cassie.* Her eyes were wide, filled with terror. He again covered her hand, but this time it wasn't to comfort her. It was to pray. He put his hands together, mouthed the word *pray*, and she nodded. Their heads came together, their helmets clanging against each other, and he shouted the words that came from his heart, as he thought Cassie was doing, too. It was impossible to hear each other, but he knew that it only mattered that God heard them. He couldn't tell if minutes or hours had passed; all he knew was that it was a place of respite from the turbulent ride.

With zero warning light flooded the helicopter. They straightened up and he looked around. Sunshine! They were in the clear.

He looked out and saw that Sean had maneuvered them away from the storm, the dark mass of clouds still swirling above them and to the east.

"Whoa! Way to go, Sean!" he shouted but didn't slap the pilot on the shoulder, as he normally would. Sean didn't need the distraction.

Daniel smiled at Cassie and saw the joy on her face, as well as the tears that streamed down her cheeks. He'd never seen such a perfect expression of gratitude, of beauty, before. Something yanked at his heartstrings, deep down inside. He didn't want to examine what might be happening here, in this helicopter, heading toward the farthest reaches of civilization. It was time to go over why he'd come back to the Torngats in the first place, mentally prepare for when they landed at Base Camp.

Without warning, the helicopter began to swirl in a circle, as if an invisible hand had swiped them across the sky. Sean yelled, his voice a wisp against the horrible noise ratcheting through the aircraft. Daniel grabbed for the safety handle next to him and watched as Sean fought to regain control. He looked outside, seeking any kind of landmark, but only saw trees and a large irregularly shaped aquamarine lake. The helicopter was flying at an unnatural angle, losing altitude as it spun out of control. The g-forces weren't anything like a fighter jet probably had, but they were enough that he couldn't even look over at Cassie. He tried to reach for her hand, his arm flailing with the force of their fall.

Please, God. Please be with us.

He silently repeated the only words that came to him as Cassie's screams drowned out the failing motor. He looked at Sean, the controls, the view beyond the windows. They were going down, fast, and this might be where he took his last breath. Finally he felt Cassie's hand in his right hand, clasped it, and with his left he urged her to tuck her head into her knees by pressing on the back of her helmet. He did the same. And prayed.

Sadness competed with panic as Cassie's heart raced inside her chest. She was going to die in the same mountains that had taken Great-granny Eugenia. Grandma Rose would never have closure. What a macabre way to honor a family legacy!

As she scrunched down, head pressed into her knees, she'd never known such terror, and yet, there was nothing she could do. Daniel and she had prayed together, and she knew she should continue now, but she couldn't find the words as her brain screamed at her to do something, *anything*. She'd never experienced such a sense of complete powerlessness.

God, protect us!

The helicopter slammed against what felt like a brick wall. She was certain the frame would break apart but instead it felt as though they were slipping down a very rough amusement park slide. And then…nothing, as they floated, or fell—she wasn't sure which—her stomach sinking again and again. Until another hard shudder made her jaw bite down, hard, as her helmet bounced against Sean's seat in front of her.

The silence that filled the helicopter as soon as it stopped moving struck her first, followed by the eeriest stillness. The helmet did its job, as she was still conscious, the crash leaving her unable to move right away. She was still here, still breathing, and this definitely wasn't a nightmare. She was in a downed aircraft, and her next step had to be to somehow move.

"Quick, get out. Take off your helmet." Daniel's sharp command gave her something to focus on. He was unbuckling her, forcing her to sit up. He'd already removed his, unstrapped his restraints. Once she took off her helmet, she realized why he was so stern, moving with grim purpose. Water—they were under water, save for two or three inches of the window that revealed a cloudy sky above. Her head got turned and she faced him, saw the steely flickers in his eyes. "Do you understand me?"

"Yes!"

"We're going out of my door. I've got to let the water come in, to even the pressure, before I can open it. Take your last large breath right before the water hits the top of the cabin. Hold your breath and do not give up. I'll lead us to the surface. We're getting out, Cassie!"

She nodded and mentally clung to his voice. They were going to live. She'd survived a helicopter crash!

"Sean! We have to help him!" She wondered if he was getting ready to exit the helicopter, too, but couldn't see him over the tall seat back. Daniel was already leaning across the cockpit seats, his arms reaching toward the slumped figure. When he sat back down the stony set of his mouth struck fear in her. Was Sean dead?

Go, go, go.

Water began to pour into the plane and Cassie's doubts, and certainties of her demise, too, returned. Her feet, legs and waist were weighed down and she couldn't wait.

"I've got to get out of here, now!" she screamed and pushed at Daniel. Her mind had zero mastery over her instinct, which told her in no uncertain terms that death by drowning was imminent.

"Wait. Only a bit more. Start taking deep breaths, hold them, force them out. It'll allow your lungs to expand as fully as possible." His eyes where steady on her and she didn't want to look into their depths, didn't want to stay still. Not one. Second. More.

Daniel's hands grasped her shoulders. "Look at me, Cassie. Get ready to take a deep breath. One, two, three, now hold." His gaze, full of confidence and expertise, was the last thing she saw before they were fully under.

The water rose above them and surprisingly, it was clear. She made out his profile, saw the light pour in from the side. Just when she thought she couldn't hold her breath any longer, Daniel turned and opened his door. He pulled her out, his strong hand holding her by the wrist. She went, kicking past the door, and swam up to the light.

They broke the surface and Cassie sucked in the air, wanting to cry with relief but that would take too much precious oxygen. As she made to tread in place, she realized her feet were touching the bottom of the lake; at a steep incline she let her feet climb as her hands paddled toward shallower depths. She was freezing. It was like moving through ice, the cold freezing her in place, but she made it to where both feet were on the lake bottom, enabling her to straighten. When she stood the water rested at her waist. They had somehow landed on a shelf; the clear water revealed the bottom, and then the much deeper blue toward the center of the lake. Where the helicopter's nose was submerged.

Daniel stood a foot from her, mouth wide open, hands at his sides, catching his own breath. Unlike her, he was scanning their surroundings, his gaze keen. He pointed. "There's the closest shore. Can you walk there, Cassie?"

She looked where he indicated and saw the edge of the lake. "I'll try." Shivers shook her body and she knew enough about hypothermia to understand she had to get ashore, fast. "B-b-but S-S-Sean." Her teeth chattered. The crashed helicopter was behind them, the tail pointing up and the front rotor tilting toward the deeper part of the water at a sickening angle. A deadly angle.

"I've got him. Go, now!"

He didn't wait to see if she listened but dove back, toward the front of the helicopter. She would have screamed at him to stay if her chest wasn't working so hard to keep the air coming into her lungs. Cassie wanted to help Daniel and Sean, but knew she'd be of more use alive, which meant she had to get out. Before Daniel had to rescue her, too.

The image of her limp body floating into the deadly depths of the lake struck her and she forced it away. No! Cassie had a life to live for, a family to return to.

"Thank You, God. Thank You, thank You." She

spoke aloud, using the prayer to remind her of her faith, that God had gotten her this far, to keep going. Never give up.

It took far longer than she'd ever have imagined, to move what she estimated couldn't be farther than one hundred yards, to get ashore. As her body rose inch by inch from the cold, the saving grace was that the air was a fraction warmer, but not by much. When she finally dragged her legs out of the lake and her feet hit the rocky ground, her knees failed and she collapsed, unable to keep her grip on consciousness. Her last thought was of Grandma Rose.

Please forgive me.

Certain that Cassie was headed toward shore, Daniel went back to the helicopter to try to see if there was any chance of saving Sean, acutely aware of his narrow window to do so. Daniel had mere minutes before he'd be too cold to move, and no way would he leave Cassie alone in this wilderness.

He approached the aircraft from the other side, as its nose pointed directly opposite the shore. Dread filled him as he saw the helicopter was slowly but certainly sinking farther. He was up to his chest now. Reaching the pilot's door, he saw Sean. His head was at an unnatural angle, his skull cracked open, his eyes unseeing. All indicative of a mortal wound. To make certain Sean was beyond help, Daniel pried open the door, just enough to fit his arm in. He felt for a pulse at the jugular. Nothing moved beneath his numb fingers, and Sean gave zero response to the rough examination.

Could he make an attempt to retrieve the body? He

knew if it was his brother or father, he'd want to have their remains. But Daniel had taken enough survival training courses, and given them himself, to remember one of the first rules. He had to do everything to make sure he and Cassie survived, since they already had made it through the crash. If he opened the door any farther, he risked sinking the craft faster. The fact that there was nothing he could do for the fallen pilot, and that the helicopter was going to sink into what was an incredibly deep lake carved by glaciers eons ago, made the decision for him. He looked up to the sky, beseeched God to give him the courage to take his next steps.

He already knew what he had to do.

Going to the cargo access door, still slightly above the waterline, he opened it and pulled out all of the bags, including Sean's weathered duffel. Daniel knew that in the wilderness anything could become a lifesaver and chances were that Sean had at least signal flares with him if not a rifle. He slung his and Cassie's backpacks over his shoulders with Sean's, and grabbed the smaller but surprisingly heavy bag that Cassie had brought. Normally the extra weight of their belongings would be of little concern, but he could feel his strength and stamina ebbing away, being soaked up by the mountain lake's chill. A dull ache had settled in his thighs and he wondered if he'd cut them on the helo or rocks. Daniel's limbs grew heavier than the luggage indicated. But fear of dying in three feet of water at the edge of nowhere propelled him forward, toward shore, toward the woman who needed him.

Chapter Three

"Come on, Cassie. Talk to me. Wakey, wakey." Firm, cold hands gently slapped at her cheeks and Cassie groaned in annoyance. She'd been in a place with no fear, no terror and no cold. *Freezing.* She was colder than she'd ever been. Ever.

"Wh-wh-wh—" Cassie couldn't get her mouth to form words. But her eyes opened, so at least her lids weren't frozen shut, and she again looked into the nicest pair of eyes, maybe ever. Warm emotion swirled into her awareness and she wanted to thank him. But she couldn't even tell him that, because she was about to die of the cold. So many thoughts chugged through her brain, as if it was made of gelatin and hadn't been utilized in years.

"Don't try to talk. That's it, you're doing great." She was propped up and watched as Daniel took off her jacket, talking to her the entire time. "You are safe with me, Cassie. But we've got to get these wet clothes off of you. I have to get the rest of mine off, too. I have dry clothing in my backpack, enough for each of us.

You will feel much warmer the minute the moisture is off your skin."

"Okay, okay. I'm okay." She climbed from the seated position he'd helped her into, and onto all fours. "Let me stand." He supported her forearm and miraculously, her legs worked. The warmth of the sun on her face was a promise for how the rest of her body would feel as soon as she rid herself of these wet things. Daniel was right—the way to getting past this uncontrollable shivering was getting her clothes off.

In front of a total stranger.

"As soon as you feel steady enough, I'll get my towel from my backpack." He nodded toward the edge of the lake, where water met shore. Her backpack stood next to her smaller bag, Daniel's large-framed one and a second duffel that she recognized as Sean's.

"But—"

"There's no one for miles, and I'll keep my back turned to you until you tell me you're dressed. I have to get the rest of my clothes off, too." He must have recognized the trepidation in her expression. Belatedly she realized that Daniel already had removed his jacket and shirt. Unlike what she'd seen in the movies or read in books, there wasn't an iota of romantic sparks between them as they were in a race to survive. She knew that the latter thought was somehow funny but couldn't grasp at the humor just now. Her brain was slow but still working, for which she sent up a prayer.

"I'm g-g-good." Her teeth chattered in time with the shivers wracking her body and she made for the low brush that grew past the rocky beach. "I'll be undressed in a flash."

"Here are the dry clothes."

Walking wasn't as much of a given with legs that felt more like heavy weights. The pain of pins and needles was edging in, and while she knew it was a good sign, she also understood it was only going to get worse before her circulation fully returned.

Neatly folded clothing was placed in her hands. It was some of the base layers she'd packed in watertight bags. She'd been worried about a rainstorm soaking her duffel. "Hurry, Cassie. The sooner you're dry, the warmer you'll feel."

"I know. I can do this." Her words came out in gasps. Where was the stamina she'd worked on so diligently in cycle class at her gym? It felt like forever until she was behind the large boulders, Sean out of sight.

"I'm at the water's edge and I promise I won't turn around until you give me the word." His shouted words reached around the pile of massive rocks. She didn't turn around, didn't answer back. Cassie needed every ounce of energy and focus to get the task at hand done.

Never had changing her clothes been so painstaking. After what felt like hours, she finally managed to change into her long underwear and thick hiking socks. The soft, warm fabric was lovely on her skin. Rubbing her hands together, she stomped her feet as she walked back to Daniel.

Lovely? What was she thinking? This wasn't a spa day with her BFFs. *Please, God, help me. Help this nice man. We are in danger.* Indeed, the gravity of their plight increased her anxiety in proportion to her thawing out.

"How are you doing?" Daniel's query gave her a reprieve from the mental tailspin, jerked her out of the sense of impending doom.

"Good. I'm dressed." She saw that he'd changed into different clothing, too. He held wet pants in his hands and there were dark stains on the legs. "Did you hurt yourself?"

He shrugged. "Nothing major. A few cuts. I cleaned and butterflied them while you changed."

She knew she'd be complaining if she'd broken skin. This man seemed strong as an ox. And he was trained in first aid, apparently. "I've got a first aid kit, too, if you need anything else."

"Good to know. Let's get to work."

She turned and couldn't help her stomach from sinking at the harsh reminder of how close they'd come to death. If her family found out about the crash or figured out that she had missed contacting them as promised once at Base Camp, they'd be worried sick. As soon as they figured out their options, she'd ask Daniel what the best way to contact home would be.

Surrounded by mountain peaks whose caps were hidden by clouds, she inhaled until her nostrils filled with the pure, clean air. No matter how much she strained to hear, she only picked up the occasional bird chirp amid the constant wind. Everything she noticed underscored that they were far from civilization.

Daniel wasn't wasting time taking in the scenery, though, as he paced from the brush to the beach, creating a pile that she assumed was for a fire.

"What can I—ouch!" The shore was full of sharp stones. She bit her tongue as her leg jerked up, not wanting Daniel to think she was a wimp, no matter that a sharp stone had dug into her sole.

"Watch it, the last thing you need is a cut foot. Here, give me a sec." He jogged over to his backpack and pulled out a pair of flat athletic shoes. "Here you go. They're for rock climbing, but they'll get you through until your boots dry out."

"I've got my hiking boots."

"And they'll need to be dried, along with all of the clothes you just took off. Let's get a fire going, then we can lay everything out."

"But what about Sean?" As she warmed up her thoughts began to fire. She swung her gaze again over the impossibly beautiful mountains, harsh and rugged, that surrounded the pristine aquamarine lake, shots of bright blue sky through the heavy cloud cover teasing her with the promise of better weather. Nothing to indicate they'd ever been here.

"Wait—where's the helicopter?" She stared at the water, as if her memory was able to will the aircraft back to the surface. Will the pilot who'd so adeptly maneuvered the failing flight so that she and Daniel lived to emerge.

"Sank. Sean didn't make it." He kept working, stopping only long enough to nod at the shoes in her hand. "Put those on." Was it her cold-addled brain or was Daniel behaving more like a robot than a human being?

"Hold on. How could the helicopter sink so quickly? At least a part of it was on the shore shelf. We were able to wade out of the lake. And even if Sean's...dead... we have to save his body!" At some level she'd already known Sean hadn't survived. A memory flashed and she saw the pilot's head hitting the flight console. It must have been when she'd been certain they were all going to die. The gravity of their experience hit her again, and she wondered just how many other memories would return to torment her. She'd heard of survivor's guilt but never before experienced it. Her insides tightened into a thousand tiny fists and she scoured her mind for anything she could have done to change Sean's outcome.

You're not in control.

No, she wasn't. And Cassie had no doubt God was with them, taking them through every step of this disaster. But she didn't have to like a bit of it, did she?

Gratitude is an outcome of faith. Grandma Rose's oft-said words quieted her racing mind, eased her heated emotions.

She wiggled her fingers, her toes. Pinched the skin on the top of her hands. *Thank You, God.* She was still alive. Shivers returned, but now they were triggered by her emotional vulnerability instead of the cold as she processed how differently the crash could have turned out for her, for the man she realized saved her life. The *men* who'd saved her life. Sean had guided the plane to the safest spot he could find, and Daniel's quick actions and confidence had given her the impetus needed to get out of the water in time.

She looked at Daniel. He worked away, his focus intentional, his movements precise, and while hurried, without panic or worry.

Daniel threw several boughs onto the pile he'd amassed before he turned to face her. He was dressed in what she recognized as high-tech all-weather clothing similar to what she'd packed: a long-sleeved top and what looked like the pants he'd had on earlier, only in loden green instead of charcoal. He had worn athletic shoes, probably a spare pair as he'd given her what looked like newer ones. He stood at the kindling's edge and studied her as if she were a complete novice. Heat rose in her cheeks, but instead of being grateful for her blood doing its job she wished she could scrub her cheeks of the evidence of her emotions. Daniel didn't seem like a man who entertained feelings. Not when he could say their pilot had died in such a matter-of-fact way.

"The lakes around here, a lot of them, were formed by glaciers. The lake beds drop precipitously. We were okay because we got out on the right side of the helicopter. If we'd taken the other door…"

"We would have swum to the shallow part."

"We would have tipped the helicopter into the depths all the sooner. As for swimming out, in that cold water? We're blessed we were able to walk out." A brow raised in disbelief. For the first time since she'd met him, Cassie thought that he wasn't the nicest man at all. In fact, he was being downright rude.

"I'm not the inexperienced hiker you think I am. And for the record, we're blessed we made it out okay." As far as Cassie was concerned, only God's grace had allowed for their ability to make it this far.

"Hiker?" He deftly ignored her reference to anything remotely spiritual. Where was the man who'd prayed so earnestly with her as their lives appeared to be over?

"That's right. I hike on my days off. I've done most of the Appalachian Trail in Pennsylvania, and I've been all over the PA Grand Canyon." If she expected to see his expression change to one of being impressed, the way the lines on his forehead deepened clued her in that it was an unrealistic hope on her part.

"I appreciate that you think you enjoy the outdoors. Let me guess, you usually day hike, staying in your car or a cabin at night?"

Actually, she usually drove home and slept in her cozy bed. Not something she was going to admit to Daniel when he was acting like this.

"What difference does it make? I'm trying to tell you that I'm not someone who's never had to deal with roughing it. Tell me what you need me to do and I'll get it done."

Daniel's face remained neutral but his dark eyes revealed a storm. As much as she had no doubt of his wilderness expertise, it was telling to see the struggle in his gaze. Fear speared through her indignation and she wished she could close her eyes and find out this was no more than a nightmare.

"I'm sorry, Cassie. I've got a million thoughts racing through my mind, all focused on staying a step ahead of the weather and the elements."

Compassion welled in her chest. This man had saved her, himself, and managed to get their luggage ashore. Who was she to judge him? Her defensiveness cracked. She let out a shuddering sigh. "I'm the one who's sorry. We don't know each other. We've both almost died, and now we need to rely on one another. It's a lot, am I right?" She rounded her shoulders back. "I'm not the wilderness expert you seem to be, but I'm the best organizer you'll ever meet. Give me a task, and it'll get done. What's next?"

His tall frame didn't move and neither did his gaze. Daniel's focus didn't waver from the lake, his thoughts as inscrutable as the wreck far below the surface. A wreck that was buried forever in all likelihood. Goose-flesh rose on her forearms underneath the long shirt.

"Daniel?" Maybe he was having his own moment of thoughts spinning out of control.

"Before we do anything, we have to say a prayer for Sean."

Daniel's quiet words took her breath away. While she'd been busy assuming he was an uncaring automaton, he actually hadn't dismissed their pilot nor his tragic ending. The man who'd prayed with her in the helicopter earlier was back, and in fact, had never left. He'd been behind his own defenses, just as she had. If not for her faith, she'd feel ashamed by her behavior, her thoughts about him. But she knew that she could use this as a learning tool, and a way to get to know Daniel better. To support him in his efforts. This wasn't an easy time for either of them.

She'd never come this close to dying, never witnessed another's passing. While she hadn't seen Sean take his last breath, her memories of his last moments were close enough. The horror of what he must have experienced rattled her attempts to hold on to her faith that all would be well.

It appeared that she'd better take a good look at herself before she misread Daniel again. She'd experienced something she'd never shared with another human being before. They'd faced death and survived. Fear shuddered through her, making her colder than the water or wind had. She suspected there were going to be a lot more lessons learned before they were rescued. When they were rescued. Cassie sighed. It was really *if* they were rescued. A truth she loathed admitting.

Please, God, let us get through this alive.

Daniel took Cassie's hands and they prayed together for a man they'd known all of forty minutes. Yet he knew they'd be called on to tell the story of how Sean had died in the bravest manner; fighting to save all of their lives.

"Amen."

"Amen."

He released Cassie's hands but she hung on for a second longer, giving him a quick squeeze of reassurance before letting go. "Thanks for doing that, Daniel. I don't know where my priorities went."

"We just survived a fatal crash. It's only natural to forget about anyone but yourself. It's how we're wired."

"I suppose so." She rubbed at her elbows, still warming herself up.

"Are you still shivering?"

"No, not from the cold. It's actually a lot warmer than I expected." Her cheeks were the color of the sugar maple trees in autumn on the land he hoped to buy after this trip. Rosy, chafed from the cold and ordeal no doubt, but still appealing. Contrasting with her deep blue eyes.

He laughed. How was it possible to have this joy bubble up through the serious situation they were in?

"It's all relative. You sound like we're on a Caribbean island."

"Believe me, right now I'm wondering why I didn't pick a tropical destination for my vacation. Except... except I made a promise to my grandma."

"Tell you what. I'm very interested in that promise, and we'll have a lot of time to talk about it as soon as we get the fire going."

"Shouldn't we put a call out, to emergency services or something?"

Dread wound around his heart. It had to be because he fully understood their predicament, had no illusions that it might be better than it looked. Not because he didn't want to disappoint Cassie. "Sean sent out a Mayday when we first hit the cloud front. He would have recalled it when we stabilized, but—"

"But then the helicopter broke apart. That's what happened, isn't it?"

"We'll never know, but yes, I think something catastrophic went wrong with the rotors, precipitated by the bad weather. It was out of Sean's control. In fact, I think he did all he could to land in the lake, knowing it was the only chance we'd have of getting out alive. If we'd crashed against the mountainside, or into the trees..." He didn't need to finish his statement. Didn't want to. Didn't want to put Cassie through more than absolutely necessary. Neither of them needed it.

It was strange that he barely knew her and yet her safety, her well-being was his top priority. It seemed natural to be protective of Cassie. He'd have to think about it later.

You can pray anytime. His mother's words echoed in

his mind. Sure, he knew that in theory communication with God was meant to be an all-the-time deal. Recalling memorized prayers from his childhood came naturally when it looked like they were going to crash in the helicopter. But he'd let go of the long talks he used to have with God years ago.

Maybe it's time to begin again.

Cassie's eyes narrowed as she surveyed the surrounding land. Past the brush, into the tree line that was only dwarfed by the sheer rock faces of the Torngat Mountains. "We would have been blown to smithereens." No holding back. He liked her forthrightness.

"Yes."

Her blue gaze searched his face. "I know you think I'm a wilderness newbie, and yeah, I suppose I am, in many ways. But for what it's worth, my phone is in a weather- and water-proof casing. It's in the smaller bag you pulled out with my duffel. I'll get it and we'll be able to call for help."

"That's great, and if we ever get in range of a cell signal, it'll be useful. But this far from Base Camp, the only thing that will work is a sat phone. I have one with me, but do you see that fog coming in? It won't work through that."

Her eyes widened and against the backdrop of the lake he saw her eyes were a deeper blue than he'd first noticed. With specks of silver gray, not unlike a snow-capped mountain. "That's bizarre. I mean, that in the twenty-first century, with all of the available technology, we're truly stranded. Someone has to be looking for us."

"If they get the helicopter's signal, if they heard

Sean's SOS, yes, someone will come looking. Eventually, when the weather clears. By all indications there's going to be snow between here and Base Camp within the next day or two. Chances are good that the weather is keeping anyone from looking for us. We can try the sat phones—I have one and there's one in Sean's bag, too—as soon as the fog lifts. But we can't sit here and wait for that. We'll end up dead. We're going to rest for the night as dark's falling soon. At dawn we begin our walk out."

"If our cell phones can't send a signal, how will you know where you're heading? How are you going to know which way to go? How do I know you really know what you're doing, that you're not taking us to our deaths?"

He stared at the woman whom he'd come to value a lot in a short amount of time. In only a matter of— he checked his fitness band for the time—eight hours. "You don't. You're right. I could be making it all up. As I see it, there isn't much choice here, is there? I downloaded maps of the area before I left home, just in case. They're on my phone, still accessible."

"Until your battery runs out."

"I had some maps printed and laminated, too. And I have this." He pulled his small, round compass from his jacket pocket. "I know we need to travel north, north east. NNE."

Her face brightened a fraction and it released some of the tension in his chest.

The fog encroached across the lake and the temperature was noticeably lowering. He needed to get the fire going. Cassie's shoulders moved and he saw her shiver. Instead of complaining, she laughed.

"In truth, some folks pay big money for this kind of adventure, don't they? No disrespect to Sean, of course. Look at me like a student, Daniel. Whatever you want to teach me about wilderness survival, I'm ready to learn." Her attempt at levity struck him somewhere in his center. In the midst of life-threatening weather and surroundings, Cassie dug deep and found a reason to keep going. The positive side. He could learn a lot from her.

"This light's only going to keep fading. Even if the fog blows away it'll be nighttime. We've got to set up our camp now." His words smoothed the smile lines from her face and he immediately wished he could pull them back. Maybe it was time to start talking to God more freely. He needed all the help he could get to keep his wits about him.

Their lives depended upon it.

Chapter Four

"**I** need to get dry socks on. I have spares in my luggage." Cassie wasn't going to waste another minute trying to tell Daniel why she wasn't the heavy baggage she figured he imagined her to be. Instead, they just had to get on with it.

"We'll spread out all of our wet clothing as soon as the fire's nice and hot. They'll dry in no time." He repeated his earlier intention as he squatted next to the neat pile of sticks and began stripping bark off a dowel-sized branch. Cassie had watched enough reality wilderness survival programs to know he was working toward that first needed spark. From that, all the heat and lifesaving warmth they'd need would come.

"You'll see what I mean soon enough." She muttered under her breath as she grabbed her bags and hauled them across the beach, away from the water's edge. It was safe to assume she looked a bit comical, her hair a rat's nest around her head, her makeup undoubtedly all gone, balancing both bags as she tried not to twist an ankle on the uneven ground, but Cassie was on a mission. Besides, no one was looking. Daniel paid her as much attention as one of the stones she stepped so carefully to avoid.

When she came within a few feet of him, she stopped and unloaded her small duffel bag, unzipping it and dumping its contents. She proceeded to do the same with her hiking backpack, the most expensive piece of luggage she owned. She'd chosen it especially for this trip.

"I wouldn't do that until we're certain I get the fire going. It's difficult to repack wet clothing." Daniel didn't look up from where he was working a small rock and stick against each other.

"Ye of little faith, Daniel." Cassie bit her lip to keep from grinning as she waited for Daniel to glance her way. His gaze met hers and he must have seen her sense of accomplishment in her expression, because he then perused the contents of her bags. All packed neatly and color-coded into zippered plastic bags. They weren't all one hundred percent waterproof, as in they wouldn't survive hours underwater, but had just enough resistance to the dip in the lake that all of Cassie's clothing was still dry.

"You prepacked all of your clothing?"

"One bag for each day. It makes changing easier and saves so much time. You never asked what I do for a living."

He paused in his fire starting, his brow raised. "No, I didn't. Tell me."

"I'm a professional organizer." She wasn't going to tell him about her counseling degree, not yet. It might stop him from sharing about his family, his life, for fear of her analysis. And truth be told? A small part of her longed for him to ask her about herself. To care. She mentally swatted the thought away as she brushed windblown hair from her eyes. Daniel's impassive expression appeared to be wavering.

His stony face, so intent on his work and getting their survival strategy on track, broke into a heartwarming grin. "Fantastic. This is the best news I've had all day. So all of your clothing was in air-tight, waterproof bags?"

Self-satisfaction and pride in her hard-won skill warmed her insides. "Not completely waterproof, but close enough. I thought you'd appreciate that I can change into my own clothing and return yours. I would have mentioned it sooner but my mind wasn't working right. Not until I warmed back up."

"I don't suppose you have any food in there?" He was back to the rhythmic motion.

"Two weeks' worth of protein bars, nuts and individual packets of peanut butter. And chocolate, of course." She looked over her supplies, remembering how she'd packed with painstaking thought, ensuring she wouldn't over or under pack. Making certain that she'd have enough to fuel her days, no matter what kind of food the tour group provided.

"You know, that's not far off from what I've packed. Did you bring any source of carbs?"

"Besides the chocolate? Only a few packets of this goo my mother insisted I take. Oh, and some honey." She plucked the bag with her condiments from the pile. "I bought the peanut butter that has honey mixed in, too. Let's see, there are twelve packets of it."

"Smart woman."

"It's not perfect but it'll keep us from starving." She knelt down across from him. "Can I help with the fire?"

"Nope." His face lit up with relief as smoke snaked up from where stone contacted the bare branch. "Come on, stay lit." He spoke as if it were a real baby, or pet. She knew she'd never take heat for granted again, as a blaze erupted in the pile of sticks Daniel was blowing air onto. His fingers were quick as he layered wood atop the kindling, taking care to allow room for air to feed the flames.

"I'm impressed. I've seen that done on television, and once or twice someone on our hikes was able to do that, but I've never had any luck with rubbing two sticks together."

"It's a skill, is all. It doesn't hurt that I carry this." He held up a flint starter, which she knew provided a spark each time the handles were squeezed together. But Daniel still had to get the wood hot enough to combust. "I'll teach you—we'll have plenty of opportunity."

Worry sank her spirits to a new low. "You really believe we're going to walk all the way back to the base camp? Or, rather, to it? Since we never got there to begin with."

"I think it's a real possibility, yes. But you know what else, Cassie? I know that we can do it. We've gotten through something most people never face, a helicopter crash. As for the water and cold, that's something I'm always prepared for. It's basic Wilderness Survival 101. All we need to do now is stay warm, fueled and get rest each night." He said "each night" as if there would be more than a few. Cassie's stomach flipped and she took in a deep breath, held it for a count of six, blew it out forcefully. It was a technique she gave her clients for dealing with the stress and anxiety of daily living. It didn't hurt when faced with life-threatening conditions, either. After two more rounds of deep breathing, she was in a better head space to summon the courage to ask the question she knew she probably wasn't going to like the answer to.

"How far do we have to go, do you think?"

"Eighty miles. Doable in a week if we push it."

"A week? I've hiked thirty miles a day without a problem."

"In Pennsylvania?" His mouth curved in a half grin, softening what she otherwise would have thought was sarcasm.

"Hey, don't knock it. You must know as well as I do that the PA portion of the AT is considered by many to be the rockiest of the entire Georgia-to-Maine route."

"We're not in PA, Cassie. This isn't the Appalachian Trail, either. I know it's not easy, doing the AT, but you're always much closer to civilization and help there than we are here." He spoke quietly, considered her. She had the distinct impression that Daniel was measuring his words. It was both comforting—that he wanted to keep her mentally comfortable—and infuriating, that he might think she wasn't capable of handling the truth. Yet she didn't pick up any "me-man, you-woman" vibes from Daniel. He'd been nothing but forthright and honest with her since they'd met in front of the coffee machine at the regional airport. And he'd treated her like a partner, for the most part. His lack of patience with some of her remarks was his way of showing his own anxiety over their predicament, she assumed. She hadn't been on her best behavior these past several hours since they'd met.

It seemed like a year ago, not just this morning.

"I hear you, Daniel, but I'm an optimist by nature. How else could I help a hoarder turn their home into a welcome respite?" Her attempt at levity seemed hollow. "I'm unable to give in to the idea that we're going to have that much of a problem hiking out. My only concern is how we'll know which path to take, where we are at any one time, without our cell phone GPS. We can't count on our batteries to last long, especially if the temps stay low."

"I have my portable satellite GPS. If that fails, we'll survive the same way explorers and wanderers have before." Daniel stood and walked over to his backpack where he routed in the bag for a few seconds. He pulled out his hand and opened it to reveal a compass.

"I forgot about your compass. Is it going to work?" She eyed the tiny item. It looked like Daniel had found it as the prize in a box of cereal or caramel corn.

"Along with my maps, yes." He reached over and pulled out what looked like a deck of cards. Within seconds he'd unfolded a laminated map and laid it on the ground between them. "We're approximately here." His finger pointed to a spot otherwise unmarked on the map. She noticed labeled points, and recognized the airport they'd come from, the base camp they'd been headed to, and three other tiny X's. Two appeared close—within a day's hike, maybe—to where she'd planned to go with the tour group. Where she thought her great-grandmother's B-17 might be. "What are those X's for?"

His expression shuttered and he folded the map back up, placed it in his left shirt pocket.

"Nothing, those are just spots I'd hoped to explore. You're an organizer, I'm a high school history teacher." The warmth she was getting used to seeing in his eyes dissipated. As if Daniel had something to hide.

"So you're researching the history of this area?" She couldn't have kept the skepticism from her tone if she'd tried. Was it possible that Daniel was looking for the same crash site that she was? And if he was, why?

"In a sense, yes."

"If we're going to get along and help each other out of this mess, it's important that we're honest with one another. What exactly are you here for, Daniel?" As soon as the question left her mouth she realized that by asking him for his motives, she'd have to provide hers. Could she trust Daniel with her deepest hope?

Cassie's demand wasn't spoken with malice or any sense of threat. Yet in her tone he recognized the need for truth. Daniel wasn't a liar; in fact, he prided himself on being a man of integrity. But faced with someone who had nothing to do with his treasure hunt, and having had signed a nondisclosure agreement with the company that contracted him, he wasn't going to tell her exactly what he was doing in the Torngats. And he wasn't certain why Cassie was out here, either.

"I explore areas that have historical significance. I'm under contract with a company that's interested in certain landmarks, both manmade and natural. It's my job to find whatever I'm tasked with and send a report back."

"That sounds pretty vague to me." Her blue eyes reflected the flames that were finally licking up the dry branches he'd found in the forest behind them. The sun hung in the middle of two mountains to the west, just about to disappear. He'd have to make camp for them ASAP, before the fire was their only light.

"Sometimes I find something interesting, other times, nothing."

She looked down at her backpack and duffel, still open on the rocky shore. "I think I'd better get changed before it's completely dark. Do you think the fire will attract bears?"

"I'm more concerned about the peanut butter in your case attracting them. But you've sealed it all well enough that we should be okay. It won't get completely dark, not until the wee hours and only for maybe an hour. The fog's just making it seem darker, but if it was clear it would feel more like dusk. We're still in long summer days." He motioned at the boulders she'd changed behind earlier. "Go ahead and walk into the woods a bit, there behind the rockpile, past those evergreens. Use the facilities if you need to. We haven't had a single sign of large animals, so now's as good a time as any."

She laughed, and it was as if all the stress and worry of their predicament melted away. Her smile did more to light up her face and reflect what he suspected was a deep inner beauty than any fire ever could. "That's pretty funny. 'Facilities.' As if there's a fancy powder room and hot water around the corner. I appreciate your effort to make this as normal as possible, Daniel. This situation is awkward enough."

"We'll have to take advantage of the freshwater lakes, creeks and streams to stay as un-smelly as possible." He was grateful for the excuse of cold air to make his cheeks red, because he didn't want Cassie to know how embarrassed he suddenly felt. Her comfort remained his primary concern, and basic bodily functions were all part of wilderness training. For some odd reason, though, with Cassie everything became incredibly personal. If he were on his own, he wouldn't worry so much about his hygiene, at least not until he was closer to civilization.

"Smelly is not a problem for me. Staying alive seems to be the priority, right? I'll be back in a bit." He watched her back retreat to behind the giant stones, and was puzzled by the catch in his throat, the tightening in his chest. The way it physically hurt to have her leave his eyesight, no matter how close he knew she remained. Daniel had experienced this with his former fiancée, but not at such a deep level. He was close to his family and appreciated the bonds that ran deep between him and his parents, his three brothers. A pang of homesickness hit him. But not for the absence of his family, of the fun banter he shared with James and Andrew, both younger. He wished he could introduce Cassie to them.

But first, he'd have to get them both out of the woods, literally.

There was no fighting it. He had to accept his natural, almost primal, need to protect her. He'd kept his wits through the crash, getting them safely out of the icy water. This shouldn't be hard, letting Cassie go into

nearby woods to change into her own clothing. And
yet he was more worried that ever. Bears were all over
this area, as were snakes and coyotes. Mountain lions
were a concern, too. He listened for her voice, just in
case she needed him. He was trying to have some sense
of control over the situation, and there was nothing
controllable about the vast wilderness they were in the
center of. So far from help. Memories pushed at him,
and he swore he heard his youngest brother Andrew's
screams. When Daniel was twelve and Andrew eight,
and the black bear had trundled from the woods behind
their house to feast on the birdfeeder he'd filled with
his brothers only hours before.

There had been nothing he could do to stop the bear,
to keep Andrew from almost losing his leg.

*Please, God, be with me. Help me do Your will, and
give me the strength to keep Cassie safe.*

Used to a sense of calm after prayer, panic rose in
his chest as his prayers felt shallow, superfluous. Sure,
he'd been able to pray for the repose of Sean's soul, for
them to make it out of the spiraling helicopter okay. But
to trust God with Cassie's well-being?

Not so much. Not yet, anyway.

For the first time in his life, Daniel was face-to-face
with his own powerlessness.

Chapter Five

Cassie ignored the scrape of leaves and branches against her bare skin as she took Daniel's suggestion and hurriedly changed. Surprisingly, she was beginning to warm up, even this far from the fire. Prepared to bolt toward it at the slightest indication of another creature in the area, she listened for suspicious rustlings. It was hard to believe how thick the fog was.

All of the warnings from college classes and social media about never being alone with a man she didn't know played through her mind. Could Daniel be a bad guy, a man who would take advantage of their situation? Certainly. But she trusted her gut that he was as nice and trustworthy as he'd proved to be so far. And she trusted God that He'd give her the strength and where-withal to survive whatever she was about to face. Cassie didn't remember a time in her life when her faith hadn't existed. Blessed with a believing family, she'd grown up surrounded by faith and love. Prayers were said together before meals and her father read aloud from the family Bible on holidays and other special celebrations.

What Cassie cherished most was how her family freely discussed their faith, as individuals and from a generational perspective. They gave one another room for their faith to grow, too.

Thinking of her family reminded her to send up a prayer of thanks for the strength she now drew on in the scariest circumstance she'd ever been in. Fear wasn't unfamiliar but this constant clawing at her peace of mind was. She was glad she had Daniel to work through this with. They'd get through it.

They. It was scary how quickly she'd begun to think of her and Daniel as a pair. Not romantically, although in a different situation she'd definitely give him a second glance. He was as nice and kind as any man she'd met in the church singles group, probably more so. It'd be nice to know that Daniel felt the same about her. Not that this was the time to consider it.

She sighed. It really did feel like it was them against the world. Against the Torngat Mountains and this mountain they were stuck on in particular. How blessed was she that Daniel was a believer, too?

Rustling sounded and she stilled, balanced on one foot as she put on the wool blend hiking socks she'd ordered online weeks ago. More rustling, followed by definite scampering. She let out a long sigh. If that were a bear or cougar, it wouldn't be making those high-pitched sounds, would it? She didn't wait to find out, though, as she quickly donned the other sock and shoved her feet into her boots, now dry. After making a quick jog back, she dropped into a crouch to reorganize her belongings.

"You are definitely the neatest woman I've ever

met." Daniel's comment was infused with the smile he flashed. He held a tin cup of water over the fire. She saw Sean's bright yellow emergency survival duffel, flat and empty, its contents next to it.

"Is that a rifle?" She nodded toward the items he'd laid out on the ground, close to the fire.

"Yes. I'm taking every precaution to keep it in working order for us. Only half of the bag got submerged but since I'm not sure which part of the rifle did, I'm drying it all out. Sean packed all the smart items one would need in case of trouble out here."

"I never thought of bringing a weapon, or, what's that?" She pointed at an aerosol can.

"Bear spray."

She didn't need to be reminded they were surrounded by all kinds of animals. But a deterrent for one of her greatest fears made her heart race. "I wanted to bring some but aerosol on commercial flights is prohibited. I've always done my best to stay away from bears on the Appalachian Trail. One time I saw one but it was several hundred yards away."

"Yeah, well, black bears are like bunny rabbits when compared to brown. Grizzlies."

"I know what a brown bear is. They're not in Pennsylvania, fortunately. Neither are polar bears." Contrary to how she was acting, she really had done a lot of research as she planned for this trip. Bears abounded in the Torngat Mountains National Park, and polar bears were what many extreme tourists came here to see. Cassie loved nature but she'd be thrilled to never see a polar bear in the wild, unless she was in a vehicle that could outrun the massive mammals.

"Fortunately?" His tone was teasing, and heat returned to her cheeks.

"Touché." She kicked a stone. "I was being rude earlier. I'm not a stickler for words, but I don't believe in fortune. I believe in God."

"Nothing to apologize for, Cassie. I'd bet we'll see a lot of each other's ugly sides before we're through this adventure, as you called it. And for the record? I'm one hundred percent in agreement that God is why we're both still alive." He pulled back the cup from the fire.

"What are you doing?"

"I'm going to make us some MREs I brought with me. Each requires hot water."

"Don't make me one—why don't we each eat our own food? That seems only fair." Cassie didn't want to take any of his food. He needed more protein than she did, simply by the size of him. She hadn't brought anything requiring heat. The thought of a warm meal in her belly did sound like absolute bliss about now, though.

"Nope. We pool our resources." His smile was resolute. She liked how the flames lit his face with oranges and yellows in the fading daylight. "We both need hot food, the more protein the better. Feel free to mix in some of that peanut butter you brought."

"Oh, I almost forgot about it!" She rooted in her bag, grinned when she found the packets of peanut butter. "I thought these were a good idea, as they're easier to pack than a big jar."

"I usually bring the pre-measured servings, too, but..." He appeared bewildered.

"What?"

"I forgot about them. I guess the events of the day have gotten to me."

She almost laughed at how understated he made "we almost died, we saw our pilot die, we almost died again in the cold water, we're stuck hundreds of miles from nowhere" sound. But there was absolutely nothing humorous about their life-or-death situation.

"You mean you're human?" She gently teased him, hoping to bring levity into play. His generous mouth didn't lift up in a smile, though, and she made a note to herself to knock it off with her lousy tries at joking.

"Yeah." His brow furrowed over his eyes and her hand moved to smooth it. Fortunately she was holding the box of peanut butter so she didn't actually do it and make a fool out of herself. Or scare Daniel that maybe she was the one he needed to worry about.

Embarrassment flickered as she remembered how the last man she'd dated had told her she was "awfully affectionate." After she'd reflexively brushed lint off his wool overcoat while he'd been in a monologue about how important his corporate job was. Needless to say, their single date had been their last, but she still hadn't forgotten how foolish he'd made her feel.

Unlike Daniel. He made her feel important, let her know her opinion counted. As if *she* mattered. Cassie had been looking for someone who not only appreciated her but enjoyed the outdoors as she did. After working inside client homes all day, every day, she relished being outside. Hiking the Appalachian Trail was one of her favorite pastimes but since her best friend had married, she'd lost her hiking partner. Would Daniel enjoy hiking with her?

Her cheeks were hot and not from the fire. She was grateful for the twilight. She didn't want to answer any questions about why she was blushing. A handsome guy like Daniel probably had his fair share of attention and the last thing she'd ever want was to make him concerned that she fell into that category. A woman he had to be on guard against. A woman who'd develop misguided feelings for her rescuer.

Stop it with the romantic thoughts. Now.

Daniel needed her to be a trusted hiking buddy. Not someone making goo-goo eyes at him.

Another rustling sound reached her and she froze in place. "Daniel." Her voice a whisper, she saw him take notice of whatever was behind her. "I heard something when I was changing. It sounded like a small animal, but it doesn't anymore." She really hoped it was the almost darkness, the acoustic properties of fog, that made the same noise seem like it was from a much bigger creature.

Daniel stood to his full height. "Quick, get behind me." As he spoke, he leaned over and grabbed his backpack.

"What do you think it is?"

"I've no idea but since we're in nanuk country I'm not taking any chances." Any softness she'd seen in his expression was gone, replaced with urgent concern. Other than getting her out of the helicopter and into dry clothing, Daniel hadn't shown an iota of being rushed about anything. Fear made her gut hurt.

"Nanuk?" She knew it was the Inuit word for polar bear. "I know they're here, but do you think it's really one?" Her question landed hollowly on her ears. The scariest question stuck in her throat. Why wouldn't it be a bear?

"If it is a bear, no matter the type, get ready to make a lot of noise. Here." He handed her a tiny pot and its lid.

Cassie grasped the items, wondering if this was how it was really going to all end. Would they have survived an awful, lethal crash only to be killed by a polar bear?

Cassie's fear revealed itself in how her voice vibrated and the tremble in her hands. The way he had to clench his hands to keep from comforting her with a hug was becoming too familiar. Daniel couldn't let himself get distracted. They'd made it this far; they'd get through the next few minutes. If only Sean's rifle parts were ready to go, and not still drying.

First things first.

He armed himself with the bear spray in one hand and Sean's flare gun in the other and waited by the fire. He'd been here two summers ago, when he'd found another World War II plane that an investor wanted to help get to a local town, to use as the main draw at a small historical airplane museum. He'd been with an Inuit guide, and while they'd at one point spotted a polar bear and her cub, she'd never entered their camp. Hadn't come close, truth be told. They'd seen her during a hike, miles from their campsite. Of course the Inuit guide was armed with a rifle and had carried portable electric fencing they'd set up each night. At a certain point it had seemed overkill to Daniel, but he knew he wasn't the expert.

Now he wished he'd set up the fencing he'd packed,

just in case. He'd totally forgotten about it until now. It was useless at the bottom of his backpack.

Let it go.

This wasn't the time to berate himself over not doing everything perfectly. But if anything happened to Cassie...

"Do you see anything?" Cassie's voice shook. He felt her terror as she crouched behind him and he ignored how his arms ached to hold her, to erase her worries, but no way was he going to risk even glancing at her. It'd all be moot if they got attacked.

"No. The fog's making it near impossible." The odds were against them, having to wait until the animal was upon them to identify it. "I've got the flare, and bear spray, from Sean's bag. It'll be a last ditch effort, but know that if it is a predator, we need to stand together and make a lot of noise." He kept his voice as low and quiet as possible while ensuring Cassie could hear him. His peripheral vision caught on the boulder next to them, the same rock that reflected the heat of the fire, making the modest pile of sticks a decent heat source. "Climb on the rock." He'd at least keep Cassie safe.

"What? How? It's taller than I am!"

"You can do it. You said you hike in Pennsylvania. It's no different than getting up to a hawk lookout on the AT."

She was no longer behind him but had darted to the boulder before he finished speaking. Her grunts and not a few groans as she climbed reminded him of how sore he was from the crash, too. And tomorrow would bring more pain as their muscles stiffened from today's trauma.

If you live until tomorrow.

More noise from the bushes and woods, behind the boulders where Cassie and he had each separately changed today, sounded. The hairs on his nape stood tall.

"Dear God, please protect us." Cassie's quiet but firm words spoken from atop the rock wrapped around him. Prayer—of course. It wasn't his first go-to as much as he knew it should be. Sure, when he thought they were going to crash, and when it was certain Sean had died, he'd recognized the point. But right now, in the midst of possibly facing a bear? Not so much. Yet Cassie had gone straight to it. Warmth swelled under his rib cage. It'd be nice to have a friend like her, one who encouraged faith. It had been something he'd missed with his ex-fiancée.

Daniel's family had a strong faith but it wasn't anything they ever spoke about, not anything past the basic exchange of blessings and good tidings on religious holidays. Before he went down the mental rabbit hole of self-examination, his gaze caught on Cassie's bowed head, the soft clasp of her hands.

"Amen. Amen." She said the second *amen* more loudly, and he finally caught on.

"Amen."

A huge shadow emerged from the trees and he tightened his grip on both of his weapons. If only he'd been able to keep Sean's duffel from getting wet! But it was useless wasting any energy on if's.

Cassie's scream made him jump, but so did the way it cut off. He double-checked to make sure she was still on the boulder, safe. The fog made discerning the large lumbering shape for what it was impossible until it was upon them. The form on the other side of Cassie, beyond the boulder, morphed into an oversized cervid head. Relief flooded him that it wasn't a bear, and he hoped it wasn't a bull moose. But a cow with a calf could be just as deadly. They were far from out of the woods.

He kept his gaze on Cassie, ready to run to her, but needing perspective to be able to use his weapons, too. She was in the exact wrong spot for a moose. If it spotted her, it could charge, its head even with her, able to knock her off her perch.

Daniel's jaw clenched with the ferocity of the adrenaline surge through his veins, his need to yell, to shout, to jump over and grab Cassie off the rock. He fought to remain still, keep his head cool. It was too risky to do little else. He couldn't draw any more attention to them, to her.

He'd never had occasion to think about what true torture would feel like. If he had, he'd have thought about his own well-being, how he could be physically injured. It never occurred to him that he'd discover the true meaning while having to watch a woman he was inexplicably growing close to face possible harm. Pain tore threw him, and it wasn't one bit physical.

It was from the deepest chambers of his heart.

Chapter Six

Cassie yelled at the top of her lungs and waved her arms over her head, just like she'd seen on the survival videos. Until her brain registered that the form appearing from the depths of the woods and fog wasn't a bear, or a mountain lion. Was it an elk or moose? Male or female? She cut off her voice, remembering the online videos she'd watched on extreme survival. A moose! Female.

Laughter rolled up from her belly and she clutched her arms around her middle, willing the nervous reaction away. *Please, God, help me.* She knew what she needed to do, but nothing was going to work if she wasn't willing to rely on His help through it all. The moose stopped, turned its monstrous head toward her. This close the fog didn't matter. Cassie made out one of the large eyes, their campfire reflected in its lower edges. The nostrils were as big as her hand and quivered. She stayed frozen in place, hoping the animal wasn't going to prod her with its huge muzzle. She had no defense against the creature's sheer size.

Odd, she'd thought she'd be totally freaked out if this ever happened to her. Or at least losing control of her bladder. Instead, a sense of calm purpose blanketed her, seeming to come from nowhere, not unlike how the fog had rolled across the lake and descended over them, making it feel as if this were the edge of the planet, a place out of time. A large splash reached through the moment and she understood what Daniel had done. The moose swung its head away from her, toward the sound, the seemingly slow movement deceptive. That head would knock her out cold with one swipe.

Cassie knew what she had to do and didn't give herself time to think, any chance to allow her true terror to seep back in. As the moose took one, two steps toward the lake, Cassie flattened herself and slid down the side of the rock, toward where she'd come from. Toward Daniel.

When her feet hit the ground with a decided thump, she wanted to scream all over again. The noise would draw the attention of the moose and bring her toward them again. She leaned against the rock, her belly and arms flush with it, afraid to make a move as she fought to get her breath under control. Softer footsteps sounded to her left and she moved her head infinitesimally and peeked from under her arm. Running was the last thing to do with any wild animal, but she didn't think she'd be able to stop herself if the moose was right here, on this side of the boulder. She tensed, ready to run around the rock, not caring that the creature could get around to her just as quickly.

But it wasn't the female moose. It was a smaller animal, if being her height of five and a half feet tall at its shoulders was any kind of small. A moose calf. The youngster didn't care one bit about Cassie, or the rock. It was on course to stay with its mother and walked by without incident.

Tears rushed down her cheeks, a release of relief, gratitude and triumph. She was still here, unhurt, and the moose had moved on. She turned to her right, eager to see Daniel's smile, feel the validation that she'd not become a burden to him, but had been part of a team, *their* team. A partnership that had managed and distracted their first wildlife confrontation.

His back was to her, his form stark against the smudged-out effect of the firelight in fog as she headed toward him. Before she reached him, though, he turned and closed the gap between them.

"Get back! This way." His arms were on her shoulders, spinning her around as he grabbed her hand and pulled her alongside him toward the woods. Fear hijacked her heartbeat and Cassie did the only thing she could: she ran with him.

The last thing Daniel wanted to do was frighten Cassie, or worse, hurt her. He all but dragged her back behind the rock, under a bush that grew up against its backside. There wasn't time to explain. Thankfully, Cassie didn't pick this moment to fight him or his decision-making. Or maybe she'd already figured out the same thing as he had.

Only once they were under the cover of the brush, the rock between them and the moose, did he feel secure enough to look at her. The fog made the gray twilight absolute, with only the faintest hint of illumination from the fire, on the other side of the rock. He sensed more than saw her concern, heard how she took gulping breaths, exhaling on shudders.

"You okay?" He kept his voice to a whisper.

"Yes. I thought we got rid of them." She was panting but he suspected that was more from the scare than physical exertion. She'd scaled and then climbed down from the boulder as only a person in good physical shape would be able to.

"They're here for the water. They must be really thirsty or the mother would have spent more time on you."

"I was waiting for her head to knock me over with a single swipe. She's huge." Her whispers were full of awe.

"It's hard to imagine their size until you meet them face-to-face. That was a little closer than I'm comfortable with." It was easy to admit his vulnerability to Cassie. Natural. He'd never been able to totally let his guard down with another woman, always wanted to appear as if he had his life all together with no hiccups. Now it seemed no more than a silly blustering on his part, an attempt to be what he thought he should be. Maybe he should take a clue from Cassie and let God run his life all the time, not just when he experienced fear.

"You and me both." He saw her roll her shoulders, turn her head one way, then the other. Keeping herself limber, ready to move when needed.

Silence surrounded them and the soft sounds of lapping reached around the outcropping to them.

"Is that them drinking?" Cassie's profile was intent as she listened.

"Yeah, I think so." He quickly ascertained that she had to be crouching in a squat, her back up against the rock. Her muscles would stiffen up in no time. "Here, you can move—slowly—in front of me and we can take a peek. I'm not certain we'll see anything in the fog, but it's worth a try."

"Okay." Cassie moved close to him and he did his best to hold back the twigs and branches of the over-growth, keeping a clear path for her. His arms seemed to have a mind of their own; once she was right in front of him they lowered and his hands rested lightly on her shoulders, small but strong under his palms. And no use denying the invisible thread that was growing between them. He wasn't making an inappropriate move, though, but wanted to let her know she wasn't alone, that he had her back. He'd do whatever it took to reassure her.

"Are you really okay, Cassie? That was a scary scene."

"I am. Thank you." She angled toward him and he let his hands drop, not wanting to overstay his welcome. "The top of the rock would have been perfect protection from a bear, I think, at least until you could spray it. Or fire a flare. But the moose—"

"How did you know to stop screaming?"

"YouTube." Her quick, honest admission humbled him. Would he have been as forthright in the same circumstance, or chalk his reaction up to extreme wilderness experience? He'd like to think his integrity would kick in, but his pride was good at driving his actions at times. Another example of how putting faith first would level his overblown ego. If only he'd figured this out before he'd failed at past relationship attempts!

You hadn't met Cassie yet.

"YouTube taught you well. I'm sure glad you knew what to do."

"You helped, Daniel. I would have been way more afraid if I didn't know you were here."

A warmth formed under his rib cage as Daniel realized he could stay like this all night, talking to Cassie, hearing her voice in the dark. Except, wildlife.

"We have to stay here until they leave. The mother is unpredictable." He struggled to keep fear out of his voice. Not for him. When had he become such a protective man? When had being humble ever been a priority over making sure he impressed a woman?

Since you met a certain woman in front of the lousy coffee machine at the backwoods airport.

"Can we try to catch a peek of them? They certainly weren't interested in me, thanks to you throwing that stone into the lake."

"Here, I'm taller so I'll stay behind you. Sit or kneel on the ground, whichever is more comfortable."

A short laugh left her lips. In the sound he'd heard a million times from other people, he heard something new in Cassie's. Joy. Hope. An enthusiasm for life. "I don't think I'll ever feel comfortable in any position again for a long time."

"I hear you." They were both feeling the aftershocks of their bodies hitting the lake during the crash. As Cassie sat on the ground, cross-legged, he sank to his seat, his knees bent to his chest. "It's been a day."

Another soft laugh, more happiness sprinkled across the night.

"We should probably stop talking. Moose have great hearing." No matter how quiet they tried to be, nothing was going to pass by the animal, especially the mother. Daniel was grateful it was past calving and rutting season, and that all the cow seemed interested in was getting water for herself and her calf. Something tickled him in his chest, under his rib cage. *Gratitude*.

They watched in silence as the fog thinned enough to reveal the moose at the lake, lapping up water calmly yet voraciously. The mother lifted her head and sniffed the air several times between drinks, always alert for danger. Daniel never identified with a mother other than his own, but watching how the cow appeared to live for the sake of her calf more than anything, empathy struck him. Since the crash, no, before— since he'd met Cassie and found out they were headed to the same destination, he'd had the same sense of responsibility. That his job was to keep Cassie safe. He wasn't a chauvinist and Cassie had proven she'd done her share of preparation for the journey here, more than most tourists, in fact. But she hadn't revealed why she was here, not specifically. So she was either very private, didn't trust him, or a combination of both. And yet this longing to do well by her came from deep inside him, with little concern as to her motives. For reasons he couldn't explain, he fully trusted Cassie. He grunted. Maybe it was what it took to grow his faith and become the man a woman like Cassie needed in this moment. Could he meet the challenge?

Yeah, it was definitely time to start praying more.

* * *

Cassie had to wonder if her sudden fascination with the mother moose and her babe was heightened by all she'd been through today. All she and Daniel had survived. The appearance of the moose, so startlingly wild and part of this living and breathing landscape, had shocked her on a physical level, of course. There was never a time she remembered not being intrigued by nature and all things wild and wonderful. What surprised her was how raw and vulnerable it left her, as though she was connected to the very creature that could have done major injury to her or Daniel. She wanted to chalk her emotionality up to the uniqueness of the event. In all her life she'd never been so up close to an animal she'd only seen in photos. But Cassie couldn't shake what her gut told her. This had been extra special because she'd shared it with this man.

The fact that Daniel, one fine specimen of nature— the human being category—was sitting so close to her as they both took in the precious sight before them had nothing to do with it. Did it? With Daniel at her side she felt safe, protected. Not that she wanted him to think he had to keep her safe, because he absolutely didn't need to. Cassie was willing to listen to his direction when it came to hardcore survival tactics; he had far more experience than she did. But if he didn't have that past experience, would she trust him just as much? Allow this connection to form between them? It was bigger than she was, more than anything she'd expected when she'd bought her coffee out of the vending machine this morning.

Cassie had been unable to define the exact character-

istics she'd deem essential in the ideal date, boyfriend…
or husband. Faith in God, kind, loving, and a sense of
humor were definites. And now, so were strong, coura-
geous and thoughtful. Just like Daniel. Nothing like a
life-threatening situation to make her ideal man appear!

She'd definitely examine all of this later, when she
was alone with her thoughts. When anxiety over getting attacked by a bear, moose or mountain lion wasn't
her constant companion.

Her stomach rolled and rumbled, and she covered it
with her hands.

"I'm hungry, too. We'll eat when they're long gone."

"They're herbivores, right? So we're not looking like
a tasty snack." She couldn't help trying to make light
of everything as the giggles threatened to overwhelm
her. The tension of the day was proving too much. All
Cassie wanted was to get into her sleeping bag—dry,
thanks to the extra-large plastic bag she'd packed it in—
zip it over her head and fall into the oblivion of sleep.

"No, but we sure don't want to anger Mama. And I
know he looks cute and little next to her, but he probably weighs three times what you do."

The cow quickly raised her head, her ears flicking
one way and then another. Cassie held her breath, hoping their chatter hadn't annoyed her. The moose turned
in a full, languid circle, nose sniffing, until she came
back to the water's edge and her calf. In a gesture familiar to all mammals, she gently nudged her offspring,
who turned and followed his mother's lead toward Daniel and Cassie. She stiffened, ready to scramble back behind the rock. Daniel's hand on her forearm impressed

the need to remain still. Cassie heard her heartbeat in her ears and knew the cow probably heard not only that but all of their conversation, including her stomach growling.

Yet for whatever reason, the moose didn't appear to perceive Cassie and Daniel as a threat. She walked near the campfire, sniffing about as if expecting an extra patch of grass to munch on. Cassie couldn't help but compare the animal's maternal behavior with her mother's, her grandmother's. Tears welled as longing to be with them swamped her heart.

Meanwhile the mama moose, in a move also similar to a mother's, gave a pragmatic snort, clearly unimpressed with the flames. The moose turned and slowly disappeared into the fog. Her calf followed, their steps sounding loud and large with the acoustic capabilities of the fog, providing a ground cloud that made sound travel more efficiently. It was all Cassie could do to not turn to Daniel and give him a hug in celebration for them making it through what could have been a catastrophe. At least one or both could have been badly injured, which, considering the predicament they were in, might mean certain death for both. If they couldn't get out of here of their own volition, without a signal to ask for help, they weren't going to make it.

That familiar friend from this morning came creeping back. Fear in all its ugly discomfort tightened around Cassie's chest and she found it hard to breathe. Mixed with the exhaustion filling each and every inch of her, she knew she needed to do whatever it took to distract herself.

* * *

"Can we move now?" Cassie's whisper was full of apprehension.

"Yes, I think we're okay. What do you think?"

"I think that was the least curious pair of moose I've ever met."

"When have you met moose before?" He stood and reached for her hand to help her up. The ground was slippery from the dampness of the fog. She accepted his aid, placing her hands in his as she straightened up.

"Thanks." Her hands felt warm and small in his. "I've never seen moose before except online or in a documentary. That was incredible." Her words implied enthusiasm, but her tone was flat, her face pale in the firelight. He stared into her eyes and only when she gave a little tug did he release her hands. His palms felt empty, chilled.

"No matter how unimpressed they were with our food, to me the MREs seem like a five-star gourmet restaurant fare. We need to eat. It's going to be a long day tomorrow." He hoped his voice sounded surer than he did. That it didn't betray his worries. Not over walking out of the crash site, or even of establishing contact with Base Camp or an Inuit settlement, whichever proved closer. Nor was he overly concerned about more wildlife, including polar bears. All were concerns, for sure. But their biggest threat remained the elements, the mountain. There was zero room for a navigation mistake. He'd double-check his maps, be sure to put Sean's rifle together before he went to sleep tonight. No matter how many times he mentally reviewed his action plan, he couldn't shake the impression Cassie was making on him in such a short time.

She was causing fissures in his carefully constructed approach to life. Everything he did, she pushed him, made him rethink how he was doing things. The biggest example that gnawed at his conscience was with his prayers—basic, what he thought were good enough to get the job done. Cassie seemed to pray at the drop of a hat, as if it was something she did all the time, the way he remembered his grandmother had done.

When he'd lost her as a sixteen-year-old, only four years after his brother had been injured by a bear, a big part of him had shut down and he'd learned to do what it took to get by without letting the huge hole in his heart break wide open again. Grandma had taught him to pray and talked about God and the Bible when he stopped by her house on the way home from school each day, until high school. But when she'd passed he'd been unable to cope with his grief, instead burying the hurt. Until now, he'd forgotten that he used to pray with frequency all through the day.

Cassie was challenging each brick in the walls he'd built around his heart. His grandfather had survived his grandmother and often remarked that his broken heart had never completely mended. The scar tissue over Daniel's broken adolescent heart was at once being torn off and melting away.

Why now, God?

"Are you going to have beef barbecue or meat loaf?" She'd returned to the fire and was reading off the labels of the two envelopes he'd dropped when he'd picked up the flare and bear spray.

"Whatever you don't want." He had bigger things to focus on than which MRE to chow down. Like keeping them alive tonight.

Chapter Seven

"Sleep, Cassie. You've got an hour and forty-five left." Daniel's voice reached her across the fire and through what had seemed an impenetrable combination of fabric and lining when she'd purchased her sleeping bag at the premier outdoor store. She shifted and unzipped the top enough to peer out at him. He sat with the rifle across his lap, his sleeping bag folded into a nice cushion from the rocky shore.

"How do you know I'm awake?"

"You haven't stopped moving since we began our shifts." He was right; she'd only drifted off to sleep here and there and no more than fifteen minutes at a time.

"Well, for one, it's hard to get comfortable when sleeping on top of a pile of rocks. Every time I hear something, I think it's the moose." Or worse. "And I've never been this far north in the summer before." Ever, actually. "It's hard to believe it's after midnight." She peered at the semi-nightfall around them. It would be brighter without the fog, which she wasn't sure was a good thing or not right now. Did she want to see the polar bear before it ate her?

"We cleared the spot for the campsite well enough. But yeah, if we'd had more time I would have made a platform out of branches for us instead of just the tarp." He'd pulled a tarp, a tent, and many other supplies from his backpack over the past hours. Suddenly her preparedness didn't seem so wonderful. Sure, her clothes were dry and she had enough portable food to last two weeks. But no water, no purification system or tablets, and not a tent or simple tarp. A plastic poncho from her local discount department store would have been better than what she'd brought for protection between her sleeping bag and the bare earth. Nothing. "Use my tent, Cassie."

She had declined so far because it didn't seem fair to her that he had to be up and alert, and she'd be in a tent snoozing away. He'd assured her it was totally fair as he'd be sleeping while she kept the watch.

Cassie wasn't willing to admit it to Daniel, but truth be told, she was really afraid of getting stuck inside the tent. Zipping herself up in a sleeping bag was one thing. Putting herself in an unfamiliar tent with another set of zippers between her and her freedom was another. Since the moose event, she'd become even more concerned about the possibility of bears. The way Daniel had said "nanuk country" as easily as she said "cow country" when describing where she lived in central Pennsylvania amid farmland had shaken her.

"I don't need a tent when you're awake, on watch." They'd agreed to two-hour shifts through the night until full daybreak or when the fog cleared, whichever came first. He'd quickly run over how to use the rifle, even though he planned to keep it at his side and gave her the flare gun and bear spray to do the same.

His chuckle warmed her heart as much as the fire heated her front, as she faced it on her elbow. "Cassie, the tent isn't for protection from wildlife. If a bear wants you, that tent is nothing more than a tissue to them."

"You have the electric fence up. We're safer than we were when the moose visited, right?"

"Honestly? No. The fence is supposed to be a deterrent, and it will be for smaller animals. Think coyotes, maybe wolves. Possibly elk, caribou and moose, if they aren't willing to step over it. Bears are so huge up here, it's hard to describe. I was stunned two summers ago when I saw bears so far off, yet still large."

She'd felt the same when her hiking group came upon a black bear on the AT a few years back but didn't want to share that instance with Daniel. It seemed amateur, all of her hiking experience, after what she'd witnessed out here so far.

"Still, it doesn't seem fair that I'd use your tent. You brought it, so you get it."

"I meant that you could use it to keep your bag dry. This fog isn't letting up and we'll be soaked through before another hour or so."

She mentally counted her outfits. "I have three more layers to change into."

"Good thing, because we don't want hypothermia."

"Is that your biggest worry out here? I mean, as a threat to us?" She wiggled into a sitting position, any pretense of sleep gone.

He nodded. His expression was impassive as the firelight flickering on his skin. Daniel hadn't let go of the rifle since he'd put it back together, she noticed, and kept one hand on it when he was in his sleeping bag. The moose encounter had shaken him as much as her, she suspected.

"Yeah, hypothermia will lay us flat and kill us more quickly than any wildlife. We can scare most of the animals away, frankly, or avoid them where needed. The moose ended up being fine, but if it'd been an adult bull, or that cow had thought we posed a threat to her calf, either one or both of us would be hurting about now."

"So we'll keep changing our clothes and dry the wet ones by the fire." She didn't want to talk about animals anymore. Bad enough that her mind was spinning with the fearsome possibilities that awaited them.

"That's the plan, yes. But we can't count on always having a fire, depending on where we're hiking, whether or not tinder's available."

"Looking out at those woods makes it seem there's plenty of sticks to burn."

"Right. But I've been up here twice before and looks are deceiving. A lot of this land is flat-out tundra, windswept and barren. That's why running into a bear is rarely pleasant. If they're out in the open, and we are too…"

"Why are you here, Daniel? I saw your maps." Her mind needed distraction from her fears, and it was about time he fessed up. They were in it together, thick or thin. He remained silent and she blew out her exasperation on a long sigh. "Daniel. Come on."

"Yeah?" His guarded expression annoyed her.

"We've survived a lot since we met what, twenty

hours ago? I think it's a fair question. Why are you here?" Cassie wasn't letting go this time. She had a right to know whom she was having to spend 24/7 with, in such intimate quarters.

"You're right, it's fair. I teach high school history in Pittsburgh. My summers are free, and I use them to do contract work."

"What kind of contract work brings you to the Torngats when it's open for only five weeks a year?"

He grinned. "I love a woman who's done her homework."

Cassie felt her blush from her toes to her cheeks and was beyond grateful for the darkness. "I wouldn't consider a trip anywhere without checking it out first."

"What made you pick this far north for a trip, Cassie?"

"Ah, that is a very smooth transition, Daniel, but I asked you first." A flicker of doubt scraped at her trust in Daniel. Was he hiding something from her, much as she wasn't telling him about her reason for this trip?

Their gazes locked over the campfire and she saw appreciation in Daniel's honest assessment.

"You did. I'm sorry, Cassie. I'm used to keeping my work as much to myself as possible. I actually have to sign NDAs for the contracts."

"Nondisclosure agreements? For exploring a Canadian National Forest?"

"It's what I'm looking for that's considered sensitive. I told you I teach history. I've loved all history forever, since I was a kid. But I'm most fascinated by World War II, hands down. I've been able to combine that love with these summer gigs and help locate artifacts from that era that have otherwise been missing or lost since then."

"As in a World War II aircraft?"

The shock on his face almost made her giggle, but her slight annoyance that he seemed surprised that she would be interested in history helped her stay focused.

"How did you know?"

"I'm guessing, Daniel. I'm here for a World War II aircraft. A B-17."

"Are you a history buff when you're not packing a perfectly organized bag?"

"No, not at all. I'm a family counselor by trade. Like you, I run a side gig which is my organizing business. My most passionate hobby is my family's genealogy. I love learning about my history, the legacies that have been left behind. My great-grandmother Eugenia was a WASP in the war, and ferried warcraft all over North America, as well as to and from the UK."

"That's an amazing legacy. WASPs weren't given the recognition they deserved until relatively recently. Did you know your Great-grandma Eugenia?"

Sadness pierced through the glow of wonder at their conversation. At speaking to someone who knew history better than she did, about such a unique slice of this period. At being close to, and getting to know, Daniel.

"No, that's why I'm here. She died flying a B-17 back from England in 1943. Neither her plane nor her remains were ever found. I was hoping that the tour I'd chosen would at least bring me close enough to talk to one of the locals, and if I couldn't leave a plaque for her, maybe they'd keep it and place it if the plane was ever found or its whereabouts known."

"What prompted you to do this now?" Daniel's sensitivity and perceptiveness sent a shock of confirmation through her. This was right, their being together and sharing similar interests. She felt it in her soul.

"Great-grandma Eugenia had a daughter she left behind, my Grandma Rose. I'm close to her, more than most grandkids, I suppose."

"Any reason why?"

"Besides the usual reasons? You know, how grandparents give unconditional love, pass on family traditions, teach us how to have fun?"

"Go on." He seemed to understand.

"Well, Grandma Rose is probably the real reason I have my faith. She was orphaned at such a young age, and left with a very distraught, unhappy father. I didn't know him, but my great-grandfather was mean to her. I don't think he meant to be so awful, but his grief over losing Eugenia never left him."

"Do you mean he was abusive?"

She shook her head. "No, Grandma Rose always makes it clear that he never hit her. It was more an overall negativity and neglect that hung over her childhood. I have so much respect for her. Her father died right after she graduated high school, and she used the savings he'd left her to go to college. That wasn't as common for women, back in the 1950s. Grandma got her teaching degree and retired after forty years as a kindergarten teacher. She's taught me how to keep going even when it's tough, and trust me, I've never faced any of the hardships she did. I'm surrounded by a family I love very much."

"I hope you find what you're looking for, Cassie."

"Me, too. Grandma Rose is going to be eighty-five in two months and we—my mother, my sisters and I—want to be able to give her some closure. She's in great shape, don't get me wrong, and we don't expect her to…die…soon, but my mother says we can't take anything for granted, either. Oh, my parents!" Where had her mind been, that she'd not thought of them since right after the crash?

"Your parents, like mine, have been told by now that the helicopter didn't show up at Base Camp. They'll be worried, for certain. But we can't do anything about it now, Cassie." Daniel didn't brook any false comfort, which she oddly appreciated. He never patronized her.

"I know." She'd tried to get a signal on her phone and not a single bar had lit up.

"And you've been fighting for your life. Don't doubt for a second that's what we're doing here."

How could she, when they were surrounded by lethal threats?

Worry filled Cassie's expression and when it mixed with sorrow over her parents' worrying, Daniel had to fight every instinct to not get up and put his arm around her, draw her close, tell her she never had to worry about anything ever again. But he couldn't do that, and he was in the best spot to see any wildlife that might wander too close.

"I have no illusions, Daniel. I might not be the extreme survivalist you seem to be, but as you pointed out, I did my research before I came. If we're where you think we are, eighty miles from Base Camp, then it'll be all we can do to make it there before we're stuck here all winter." She'd read the online weather history of the area. Winter in the Torgat Mountains truly began at what was considered the end of summer in Pennsylvania.

"We'll worry about the hiking tomorrow. Tell me more about Eugenia."

Wonder filled Daniel as he listened to Cassie tell the story of Eugenia's heroism. How she'd been sent on the mission when her baby wasn't yet a year old. Eugenia had learned to fly crop dusters on her family's Pennsylvania farm and had been accepted by the WASPs right after the birth of her child, Cassie's Grandma Rose. It wasn't usual for a mother or pregnant woman to sign up, but Eugenia had put her name in the hat the same hour she'd heard about the WASPs on the living room radio. Eugenia's husband was somewhere in the South Pacific at the time and ended up being involved in Doolittle's Raid. He returned safely home at the end of the war, widowed and a single father to a toddler daughter, Rose.

Daniel soaked up each word of Cassie's retelling, watching her animated face illuminated by the fire and her enthusiasm. And her unmistakable deep love for her family. The thought that kept running through his mind was how incredible his and Cassie's meeting had been. What were the odds that two people searching for the same wreck would end up on the same helicopter that ended up in a lake? He knew he needed to tell her about what he was searching for. The treasure believed to be in the aircraft, though the reality of it still being there after the crash site's rediscovery seemed slim. He held out hope, though, as there were no reports of valuables being found and turned over to the proper authorities.

"Daniel? You look distracted. Did you hear something?" She twisted in the sleeping bag and looked behind her, toward the lake. Much to his relief, the fog was beginning to dissipate.

"No, not at all. I'm awestruck, Cassie. What are the chances that we'd both be out here, possibly looking for the same aircraft?"

Eagerness shone in her eyes and the dark circles under them didn't seem as deep. "Do you really think we're searching for the same B-17? There has to be more than one up here, though, right? World War II lasted four years and there were so many planes ferried across Canada."

"Yes, but the timing you've mentioned matches the aircraft I'm looking for."

"So you know where it is?"

"Well, not exactly. I've narrowed it to two different spots, but they're both between here and Base Camp. Closer than Base Camp is what I'm saying."

"I could get to visit the actual wreckage? That's more than I dared hope." The sudden lift in her tone hit him in his solar plexus.

"Whoa, don't get your heart set on it, but yes, there's a chance we could hike by it." The last thing he wanted to do was disappoint her. "And our priority is staying alive, getting to Base Camp. If veering off course at all to look for the plane appears dangerous, it's a no-go." Disappointment roiled in his gut as he told her the truth and tried not to fight it himself. It was excruciating to be so close to the wreck, if indeed they were, and accepting that because of the crash and his drastically shortened timeline, finding the B-17 might not be an option.

"You're right, Daniel. What were the odds we'd meet up like this?" Her gaze grew thoughtful and he felt the surge of warmth in his chest that was the Cassie effect. Something he knew he'd probably not leave here whenever they left, went about their separate lives.

Careful. He'd come here to find historical treasure, not a partner. Besides, how many women would be willing to have their partner disappear each summer, for most of the summer? And Cassie was very attached to her family. She wasn't likely to be someone interested in a long-distance relationship.

What was he doing, thinking of their working together to survive as a relationship? He rubbed his hand over his face, his eyes. Gave himself a second to think.

No matter his mental defensiveness against Cassie, his heart felt as though it was becoming somehow attached to hers.

"The odds of us meeting aren't impossible. Not when we're both looking for a particular World War II aircraft. The only time anyone can come up here to search for anything is during this five-week window. I know you already know this." She'd done her research, no question.

"But?" She must have heard the resignation in his voice.

"Forget it. You're right, Cassie. I'm being a jerk. Our meeting isn't by chance, or luck, coincidence. It's a blessing from God."

"I love that! You know, we haven't talked about how we fell into prayer earlier. How we both share a similar faith." Her openness was impossible to resist.

"Listen, Cassie, I'm a believer but I've not been involved in a church for a long while. I keep thinking it's something I should do but then—"

"Life gets in the way?" She nodded, thumped her mittened hand on her chest. "Me, too! Grandma Rose and my mother are always on me to join the local church they've started going to. It has a large singles group, which I'm a member of. That's fine, but since I turned thirty, I'm feeling as if I've kind of outgrown some of that. I would like to be more committed to a home church, though."

"Thirty's not old. Try thirty-two."

She rewarded him with a cheeky grin. "Good to know I'm not the old guy here."

"You're not. And I'd like to find a church that I could make my home, too. It's probably not that unusual, at our age, do you think? Do you have a boyfriend?" As soon as the question popped out he wanted to pop himself on the side of the head. It had to be the late hour, the situation.

Cassie didn't seem to notice how forward the question was. "Nope. I did some online dating. It seemed great. It was a Christian dating site, perfect for what I'm looking for, but well, it didn't work out."

"May I ask why?" There it was, another nosy question. His mother and brothers would be laughing themselves silly if they could see this. Daniel, man of the woods and lover of all things natural, not afraid to venture into the wilderness, acting like a teenager as he asked an attractive woman he happened to be stranded with some very personal questions.

You're not stranded.

The thought came unbidden and he knew it wasn't

his own. No, he wasn't by any means "stuck" with Cassie. It was a joy to be around her, even if it aged him decades from his worry that he wouldn't be able to protect her. But they weren't alone. God had kept them safe so far—who was Daniel to question He wouldn't protect them all the way to Base Camp? Calmness infused his next breaths as he listened to Cassie's explanation.

"Jim was a nice enough guy, at least I thought he was. We dated for almost six months, until I found out he was still using the dating app and meeting other women. He always made sure they didn't go to the same church and stayed away from my mother and grandma's church." She rested her chin on her knees. "It was the kind of thing I'd expect to happen when I was younger, more naive. It caught me off guard at this point in life. I mean, why didn't he just make it clear he was only interested in dating?"

"And you wanted more?"

"I thought I did, for a little bit. And sure, I'd like my own family someday. For now, though, I'm very happy with my life as it is. It's full, my business has thrived even in some hard years for our family. My dad lost his job last year and my mom had breast cancer." She shot him a quick, soft smile. "She's good. Cancer-free. Dad found another job, something he likes better than what he did for fifteen years, in fact. But it was a scary time. I had to get genetic tests to assess my risk, as did my two sisters. Two of us are okay, but my youngest sister, Breana, has to watch it, begin her mammograms earlier."

"I'm sorry, Cassie." It made his struggles with trying to make more money to fund the land he wanted to purchase in the Allegheny Mountains for his dreams of starting an extreme hiking center seem superfluous.

"Oh, it's all good, really. As I said, we all got tested, and most importantly, Mom's going to be okay. It was scary at the time, that's for sure. But overall? A lot of good came from it. I learned early on to get the most out of each day. That's why going on this trip seemed like a no-brainer." She stood and stepped out of her sleeping bag. "I need to use the facilities."

"Don't go as far this time. I can't see a thing, so your modesty is intact." He hoped his gentle teasing would help Cassie feel safe around him and her answering smile let him know it had.

"This time I'll definitely tell you if I hear anything, no matter how small I think it is. The moose taught me well!"

He looked away, out east where the sun would rise over the far mountain range. They were in a series of parallel ridges and he estimated the lake was in between the two closest to Base Camp, which still put them farther out than he'd have wished. Worse, they had to climb up and over the mountain without a trail to lead them, forging their own way. If he thought of the hard days in store for them, he could feel despair rising in his chest.

Gratitude.

Yes. He needed to stay positive. What was the best thing about this trip so far?

Not that he would have ever hoped to crash and be stranded out here, but one thing he'd never regret about this time was getting to know Cassie. As long as he kept it in mind that this was a short-lived friendship, nothing more, he didn't see the harm in enjoying Cassie's company.

And as lighthearted as he'd tried to keep things with Cassie, as he'd said, he truly didn't believe in coincidences. It was time to put his beliefs to the test, as he'd never been in a more dire circumstance. Even with all of his and Cassie's survival gear combined, their provisions were nothing against the harsh climate and surroundings.

Getting off this mountain to safety was a long shot, but a mandatory long shot. It would take every ounce of know-how and strength they each possessed.

And all of their faith.

Chapter Eight

They hiked out of the campsite as the first smudges of gray appeared between the two sharply peaked mountains to their west. Daniel's guarded facial expression, along with his methodical way of checking his maps with his GPS, hadn't encouraged conversation. Since it was clear that he didn't want to talk about anything too deep, too personal, she'd been happy to share Great-grandma Eugenia's story. And her quest to at least leave a memorial item with the locals. But as the morning approached noon and her hamstrings began to complain from all the climbing, she needed a distraction.

"You're certain we're going the right way? Besides the fact that it's all been uphill, I mean. It seems to me we should have reached the peak by now. The highest mountain here is only what, five thousand feet or so?" She had to speak loudly as Daniel was several yards ahead of her, and the narrow path they made on slippery lichen-covered rock allowed zero room to hike abreast.

"That's right. But we have to remember we're on virgin ground, and it's pretty unforgiving."

"I'll say." Her knees would remember this climb for years to come, she was certain of it.

"We need to get over this mountain, then we should see several valleys and ranges laid out in front of us. From my map and GPS, it appears we crash-landed near the base of the highest mountain southwest of the camp. But we're on the wrong side—we can't get around this climb."

"Of course we can't," she mumbled under her breath, or so she thought, but the brisk wind carried words farther than she wished.

"No time for complaining. We have to stay positive."

"It's hard—whoa!" She almost headbutted Daniel in his chest when he abruptly stopped and turned, her focus on the ground.

"Here. Take a break." He tugged her water bottle from the side netting of her backpack and handed it to her before reaching for his own. They'd filled their bottles with liquid he'd boiled over the fire last night. She was fairly certain, as was Daniel, that the fresh lake water would pose no problem without purification, but neither of them was willing to take a chance they didn't have to. Stomach upset and resultant dehydration was to be avoided at all costs, up there with hypothermia.

"How's your base layer?" She referred to the long underwear they'd both donned this morning, a fresh layer of clothing and moisture-wicking fabric.

"Good, but I know I'm sweating. You?"

"Same. I don't feel a chill yet, though." A gust hit them and she closed her eyes, turned her back to the wind. "We need to keep moving to keep it that way."

"We will." His brown eyes glittered amber with the

reflection of the clear blue sky that domed over them. Daniel pulled out an energy bar, opened it, and took half before handing it to her. "Here."

"Thanks." She chewed the date-and-nut bar. "You know, this tastes almost as good as that meat loaf last night."

Daniel nodded. "Amazing what limited choice and unlimited fresh air can do to appreciation."

"Daniel, I don't mean to pry, but can we keep talking about ourselves? I told you about my life back home. What's your faith and family life like? You touched on it last night. I really appreciate that we were able to pray together when things got dicey. It made a big difference. Without you there, praying with me, I don't think I'd have been centered enough to get out of that helicopter." The strength of his hands as he'd held hers, the immediate bond they'd been forced to form, had steadied her enough to be able to talk to God. She knew she'd have shouted out, asked for help, but would she have been able to still herself enough to feel the unconditional love that was always hers for the taking?

"Good question. And you're not prying." He chugged more water. "I grew up going to church on Sundays, Vacation Bible School in the summers. My parents were really good about saying grace, and they are truly the salt of the earth. I'm so glad to have them. They keep my brothers and I on track, that's for sure."

"Do you ever attend church now?"

"Only at the holidays, or if I go with my parents on the odd weekend I'm around on Sunday. Like you, I keep meaning to join my local church in the suburb I live in, but work and life keep getting in my way." He shot her a rueful glance. "Sad excuses, aren't they?"

"If they're sad, they're the same ones I have. Like you, I was brought up with a faith, and it was more than religion. I do believe. And I try to pray every day. But the crash, even that silly moose pair, they've got me thinking that I shouldn't wait to do anything anymore. If—" She faltered and tears welled, spilled over. Mortified, she swiped at her cheeks, and couldn't look at Daniel.

"If?" he gently prompted, and she risked a look at him. No condemnation or pity. Daniel waited for her response with quiet reserve, his face relaxed and his focus on her.

"I was going to say 'if' we get out of here, but I mean 'when.' When we get back home, I'm going to sign up at the church my family goes to. I could pick my own— that's what I was waiting to see, if I'd prefer another— but our church has everything I need."

"Including the singles group?" He was teasing her again and she welcomed the distraction from her anxiety over their situation.

"Yes, including the singles group. I placed an ad for both my counseling and organizing services in the church bulletin several months ago, offering a discount to anyone who mentions it, and have received several new clients. People tend to spill their guts when you're sorting through their lifelong accumulation of stuff, and I've been so blessed getting to know each and every one of them. That's the best recommendation I could hope for, for the right church for me."

"Hmmm." He screwed his water bottle closed and

shoved it into its pocket. "That's a good idea. Several of the other teachers I work with attend a church that's just down the road from my condo. All of them are around my age, our age—" he winked "—and they've invited me to several functions. Disc golf has been my favorite so far."

"Disc golf?"

"Instead of a ball and clubs, you throw a disc to a target point for each 'hole.' It's a lot of fun."

"It sounds like it. So are you going to?" She met his gaze and couldn't help smiling. Daniel did that to her.

"Going to what?" His false innocence was comic perfection.

She laughed, and after a heartbeat Daniel joined in.

"Am I that obvious?" He smiled at her.

"That you're avoiding the question? Absolutely." She wondered if something had happened in his life to put off committing to a home church, or if, like her, he'd simply let life get in the way.

"I'm not ready to say I'll definitely join. But I have time to think about it. Ready?" He tightened his backpack straps and she followed suit, grateful she hadn't skimped on a lower-quality model when the tour guide suggested they bring a very "hike-worthy" backpack.

"I am. Let's go."

"Tell you what. You go ahead this time. I can see over you, and it's your turn to set the pace."

"I don't want to slow us down, Daniel."

"And I don't want to wear either of us out to the point that we're too exhausted to set up a proper camp." He looked around them, at the sky, the ridgeline to their south. "Too bad we didn't have this visibility yesterday."

"We couldn't help the front coming through, and besides, that's done, over. We only have today to worry about." She didn't mean to sound so harsh but Cassie knew she had to keep herself in the present or she risked her anxiety and fear coming back, making forward momentum, mental and physical, impossible. "We're alive, Daniel. And maybe the clear skies will allow your sat phone to work."

"It's not about the weather as much as our location. From what I see on the map, and where I think we are, there's no chance of reception for at least another thirty miles."

"So by tomorrow?"

"Depends. Let's go." The guarded look had a hold of Daniel's expression again and Cassie knew him well enough to recognize his all-business mode. Her heart swelled with gratitude, and something else, affection? *Careful.* It was as if her heart hadn't been broken by Jim. As if he hadn't been a whole lot, after all.

Daniel had eased her out of the shell she'd retreated into since the disastrous relationship. She could keep talking to him, getting to know him, all day, all night, and into tomorrow. But Daniel kept on task, reminding her that all of this could be taken away with one nasty wildlife encounter. One misstep that led to a broken bone or worse. They weren't wearing hiking helmets as they'd both planned to rent them from the camp store, along with a camping stove on Daniel's part and several other items. The helmets Sean had loaned them for the flight were too bulky and didn't allow for maximum vision, so they'd left them at the lake.

Cassie stepped in front of Daniel and continued on

the trek that if his calculations were accurate, they'd only completed a tiny fraction of. Since she already felt as though she'd aged a decade overnight, her skin drying by the minute and her body so sore and bruised from the crash, she figured the farther they got each hour, the better.

Their path wasn't prehiked or tamped down like on the AT, like all of the hikes she'd done before now. All she had to follow was what Daniel told her. To keep the rock wall of the mountain to her left, and stay away from the sudden, lethal drops that appeared at intervals with no pattern, no way to tell ahead of time what was around the next curve of the mountain. She'd never experienced the unending safety of a mountain—its solid wall, its shadow, the flora and fauna that thrived on it—alongside what would be certain death. A plummet down to what looked like an endless crevice between this mountain and what she assumed was another peak to their west. All she could do was put one foot in front of the other, careful to not slip, and keep heading north.

"We can do it." She whispered it to herself, making certain Daniel didn't hear. She'd feel foolish if he heard her affirmation, that he'd mistake it as her getting worked up and worried again. Not for the prayer it was, that she had to desperately believe in.

Daniel had always enjoyed the rhythm of a hike, when he got his heart rate up enough to know he was working but not so much that he was sweating through his layers too quickly. Most often he was solo, able to soak up the surroundings, stop to take photos with his professional camera. It was a completely different situation when he was climbing for his life, and that of another. Especially that of another whom he found himself caring about more with each step of their journey.

Guilt plagued him. He hadn't outright lied to Cassie about the sat phone—it was true that it was useless until the weather cleared. Their cell phones wouldn't catch a signal until they were within range, very close to Base Camp. However, it was becoming clearer to him how much farther they might be from Way Point. As in, closer to one hundred miles than the thirty he told her. But he didn't want to stress her until he had to, until he was certain. He'd carry the worry for both of them until he had a better feel for their exact location.

Cassie had fallen silent and he was again struck by her dogged persistence, keeping pace as though she wasn't half a foot shorter than he. There was no more than an hour left in their day and he suspected she was feeling the energy drain as keenly as him. They'd already gone on for at least two, three hours longer than if daylight weren't almost round-the-clock. He needed to say something, anything, to reassure her that she was doing a great job, that they'd be at a rest point soon.

"Hey, Cass?"

She stopped and turned, her gaze locked on his, making him feel as if he was the center of her world. Until she teetered on her heels, arms flailing, eyes wide. "Ohhh!"

No.

"Cassie!" His shout shot from the center of his being, where fear and faith warred on a regular basis.

He ran toward her, closed the distance, was right next to her, but not before she fell backward. Her backside hit the rock with a frightening *thud* and she began to slide headfirst down the steep grade. Daniel lunged for her legs, landing with a sickening crunch on his stomach, but reaching in time to grasp one of her feet. On instinct he tugged until he had one hand on her slim calf, just above the ankle boot. He sent up a quick prayer of thanks that her boots were laced tightly, or he'd have lost her already, holding only her boot after her foot slipped out.

"Hang. On." He was out of breath and a sharp pain in his side made his gasps for air seem futile.

"There's nothing to hang on to!" Her yell was at least two octaves higher than her normal tone and he was instantly attuned to her fear.

"I've got you. I'm going to pull you up." He felt around with the toe of his boot until he gained purchase on a rock, then did the same with the other. One advantage to this terrain was that there was no shortage of outcroppings, large and small. The same thing that made traversing it so treacherous was going to be the anchor of Cassie's rescue.

Cassie. Pain seared through his chest and he couldn't stop to dissect it, to determine how much was physical, mental, spiritual. All he knew was that he couldn't. Let. Go.

"Daniel, I'm afraid." He heard the sob in her voice and wanted to make her safe now, whatever it took. There wasn't room for one mistake.

"It's okay to be afraid, Cassie. Use it to give you the energy you need to get back up here." As he held one calf and one boot in each hand, her legs bent at ninety degrees, he forced himself to dig deep, prepare to give this all he had. No way was Cassie going over.

"Daniel? I didn't tell you, but I hate heights. I mean, I—I…" She broke off on a moan that sliced through his heart like a bear's teeth through salmon.

"It's okay." He didn't have the stamina to keep up a conversation and save her. "Close your eyes and visualize yourself back up here on the ledge, next to me."

He felt her muscles relax, then tense, ready for action, under his gloved palms. Daniel made himself envision her back up here, safe. Looking to his left, to the mountainside, he saw the sharp-edged rocks that had been their path the last hours. Once he pulled Cassie up far enough, he could grab them with his left hand and keep a hold of her with his right.

"That's it." His voice scraped his larynx, his throat raw with effort. He dug in his toes, tried to do the same with his knees, and focused on engaging his core muscles. Slowly, slowly he tugged and pulled, until Cassie's knees were even with the ledge. He had to ignore how much she was getting bruised or cut. All that mattered was that she didn't fall. He'd spied some outcroppings, small ledges, at least fifty feet below their path but he'd never able to get her out of there, away from here. And by the time he could count on any kind of long-distance communication, she'd die from exposure.

Please help me. Please, God.

It felt like years but he got both of her knees even with her calves. His toes felt as though they'd slip at any second and he used his quads in an attempt to anchor his knees.

"Cassie, I've got you. As long as I keep most of my body on the ledge, neither of us is going to go over."

"If you have to let go, please don't ever feel guilty."

Her quiet vow cut through his focus and he froze, then burst into action. No way on earth was he letting go of Cassie. Ever.

Chapter Nine

Cassie kept her eyes squeezed shut against the dizzying view that her upside-down position afforded. All she allowed herself to focus on was the grasp of Daniel's hands on her calves. As long as he held on, she was safe, if only for right now. Heights had never been something she'd had an affinity for, and it was customary for her to hug the wall of a mountain when she hiked back in Pennsylvania. Because she knew the trails around her home so well, she usually made sure that she didn't select risky trails, choosing to go miles out of her way to avoid them if needed, unless it was completely unavoidable. And when she did have to take a more treacherous route, she did it in a group. Never alone.

You're not alone now.

Funny, she'd thought that if she ever faced death head-on she'd be freaked out, no matter her faith or beliefs. And yet, a peaceful blanket of calm seemed to settle on her, letting her think she'd be safe forever in Daniel's arms.

"Cassie, keep talking to me." His voice shattered

her mind's attempt at escape from her probable death. A scream welled up from her chest, but came out on a moan.

"I'm here. I can't open my eyes. But I mean it, Daniel. Please. Do not risk yourself any more than you have to." Cassie wanted to live, to get through this, but couldn't bear the thought of anything happening to Daniel, the man who'd kept her safe to this point.

"Listen to me, Cassie. I need you to look up here and grab my hand." He wasn't paying attention to her wishes. Daniel was a man on a mission.

"I—I can't open my eyes. Please don't make me." Terror clawed at her attempt to keep the sight of the side of the mountain, the seemingly bottomless crevice, from her vision as she kept her eyes screwed tightly closed.

The sound of a long sigh from Daniel fell around her ears. "Okay. Listen carefully. Do you go to the gym? Do you know what crunches or ab curls are?" He was speaking more quickly with each sentence, striking fear into her heart. Daniel wasn't going to be able to hold on much longer. He squeezed her legs again. "Cassie. The gym. Crunches. Can you do them?"

"Yes." It took all of her effort to speak, as the paralyzing fear wouldn't let up.

"Right. Have you ever used the machine where you hang from your legs and curl up?"

Hope sparked, tiny yet brave, in her darkest hour.

"Yes. Yes!" She saw it, looking at the back of her scrunched eyelids. She was going to do a crunch, forget about the backpack. "I think I have to get my backpack off first."

"No, there's no—just do it, Cassie. Crunch!" His shout was drill sergeant–worthy and used to her trainer's motivational tactics, her body went into automatic.

"Come on, Cassie! You can do it!"

But she was already on it, using her core to curl up, up, fighting the urge to twist to either side as she reached blindly for his hand with both of hers, her backpack impeding how far she could bend.

"Your left hand, Cassie, reach straight up. It'll be easier if you look at me."

Please, God, give me strength.

Cassie stretched her left hand as far up as she could while maintaining the crunch position, and at the last moment, opened her eyes. Eyes dark with intensity met her gaze, and she moved her arm several inches to the right, until Daniel's hand engulfed hers.

"Good going! Now, grab my wrist and I'm going to get yours."

It took all of her remaining strength and energy to follow Daniel's instruction, keeping her muscles flexed, doing a lifesaving crunch, but she was rewarded when they had firm hold of one another's wrists. She and Daniel were connected, solidly, and so far she wasn't pulling him over with her.

"We did it!" She saw the ledge they'd hiked, the mountain wall.

"Almost there, Cassie. Here we go. Try to get up here and fall onto your stomach as I pull you over. I'm not letting go."

In a maneuver she knew she'd never replicate, and prayed she'd never be in a position to use again, Cassie forced her abs to do what they'd never had to do before—lift her weight and her backpack through thin air. Somehow she made it even with the ledge. As Daniel kept consistently pulling and tugging on her arm, she got closer and closer and then above the ground. She heard his grunts, saw the perspiration dripping off his nose. It reminded her that her job was to keep her core engaged, to curl upward as much as she humanly could.

They were suspended on a crucible between certain death and survival, gazes locked.

"Please, God!" Cassie grunted around her clenched jaw. Daniel's gaze never left hers.

"Amen!" The reminder of the moose rushed hope through her. They were going to do this. They had to!

At the point where it seemed she'd never get back onto solid ground, Daniel let out a loud groan and she was catapulted onto the ledge, on top of Daniel, who had switched around to his backside and used his legs to pull her the final stretch. She saw his eyes widen in pain before she rolled off, guided by his hands so that she didn't go back over the edge. On her back, safe on terra firma, she stared up at the sky, the mountain. She was alive!

Daniel groaned again and she looked over to see him getting to his knees, his face pinched with pain.

"Did I break your ribs?"

"Naw, this is from when I dove for you. I just need to catch my breath."

Now that she wasn't preparing to die, Cassie's thoughts began to clamor. If Daniel had fractured one rib, let alone several, he was at risk for a punctured lung. They definitely couldn't afford that, with miles of hiking ahead of them.

"Go slow, Daniel."

He turned his face toward her and gave her the widest grin, full of victory and relief. "Are you kidding? I feel like I can climb this mountain barefoot about now."

"That's the adrenaline talking." She turned to her side before getting on all fours as he had, knowing they had to get upright and moving as the light faded. They were on the east side of the mountain, putting them in a dark shadow, perpetual summer twilight or no.

Her hands shook as did her knees, and the scared-out-of-her-mind feeling was being replaced with the same rush of accomplishment that Daniel described. Which would all be for naught if they got stuck up here at night, with little to no protection from the elements. The path was too narrow for a campsite. Once again on two feet, she leaned against the mountainside. "Come on, let me help you up." She held out her hand.

He gave one quick, definite shake of his head. "Too risky. This part's too narrow. I'm good."

It was all she could do to stay quiet and patient as she watched him use the side of the peak to leverage himself up. There was no mistaking his sudden intakes of breath, nor the winces that screwed his face into stony will. Daniel was in significant pain. She opened her mouth to say something, anything, to ease his discomfort. And realized there was nothing either of them could do right now, other than get off the mountain, or at least get to a place to camp overnight. Maybe they'd get a break in their struggles and a signal would appear for the sat phone. Once he was fully upright, and his breathing had regained a more normal rhythm, she knew it was time to leave.

"Are you ready? You can lead the rest of the way. Do you still think it's only another hour?" Cassie took in the lack of shadows, as the sun had already sunk past the mountaintop. It was hard to believe they had hiked all day through this terrain and yet still had limited visibility. She longed for a lookout point, a place that would give them a view of the scenery before them.

"I do. My map's accurate, and GPS confirms our location. We're almost through this awful part." He punctuated each word with a ragged breath as he leaned on the rocky mountainside, his eyes bright with honesty. "Let's do this." He turned and she eagerly followed him, anxious to be out of the mountain's shadow, clinging to them like the specter of the crash, refusing to let any of the light in.

Logic told her that worrying about his injuries was futile, as there was nothing to do but put one foot in front of the other. Very, very carefully. As they moved, she was forced to recognize again that she was sore, too, and also having a hard time getting enough air as they continued on.

The constant struggle for air could be the high altitude but she knew the highest peak in the entire range was just over five thousand feet. Altitude sickness wasn't usually a concern under eight thousand feet. But excess activity, combined with all the stressors they'd faced, had to play a factor. She suspected their breathlessness was from exhaustion, and now for Daniel, bruised or broken ribs.

All she knew as she trekked behind him, mimicking

his footfalls exactly so as to not risk going over again, was that she didn't think she'd ever voluntarily go on a hike again.

"We're almost there. I can see the end of it." He spoke through gasps, no longer caring if Cassie thought him weak. They were both hanging on by a thread of determination, and something else that he knew in his deepest being had to be God's help. He had no other explanation for how they'd survived so much in such a short time.

It had taken them days but finally, they were about to escape the mountain and area that could have been their final resting places.

But it wasn't a time to celebrate, not yet. They'd be more vulnerable in other ways, out of the shelter of the woods and in the open where dangerous wild animals were more likely to roam.

"Sunset! Let's watch the sunset." Her voice was just as raspy but it couldn't hide her enthusiasm. Cassie's constant faith had fueled them both out of the crash site and he marveled that he might never have experienced a rejuvenation of his own trust in God otherwise.

He was too beat, though, to contemplate anything deeper than placing one foot in front of the other and making it up and around this last, steepest incline. They were rewarded in a matter of minutes with the ledge opening up onto wide, level ground. The light, though dim and near the edge of the day's end, seemed incredibly bright and intense after the long hours—three full days in fact—by the mountain.

"Here we go." Daniel stopped as soon as it was feasible, where there was no chance either of them could fall off a cliff. He gestured at the view and gave Cassie the brightest smile he could muster. She stopped next to him, at the edge of a large plain that revealed the true beauty of the Torngat Mountains, spread out in waves of green, brown and charcoal in front of them.

"It looks like Scotland." Cassie's face was red, wind- and cold-chapped, her nose runny, her eyes tearing as they'd left any protection from the wind once their path had widened to the relatively flat peak. He'd never seen a more beautiful woman in his life.

They stood next to one another, the golden rays of the sun's last light reaching across the vastness in front of them. It was a great comfort to know that the light wasn't going to go all the way out, that the light would be their guide tonight and for the next several days. He estimated there was at least another week to get to Base Camp, if they weren't rescued sooner.

It didn't hurt nearly as much when he stood still, which he thought was a good sign that he'd only bruised his ribs rather than fractured one or more.

"It does remind me of Scotland, too, but I also see Norway. See that water?" He reached out and pointed to the deep blue crack in the distance. "It's part of the Nachvak Fjord, if we've calculated correctly."

"If we're right, and we both know we are, we are halfway between Torngat National Park and Kuurur-juaq National Park." She gave him a satisfied smile. They'd worked together, matching GPS coordinates to the map, plotting their path. It was satisfying to meet a woman who liked the outdoors as much as he did. He'd never dated anyone who would consider more than an hour or two of hiking.

"Bingo! You weren't zoning out when I showed our route to you."

She laughed. "No, I get that expression when I'm in deep thought. My friends tease me about it."

He welcomed the warm feeling in his chest that being with Cassie gave him. It was pure balm after the pain. A sense of well-being, knowing that he was in the right place, filled him. He'd only ever experience such serenity with Cassie, and it had been amid lethal conditions. Had it only been two days ago that she'd entered his life? It felt like months, years.

Forever.

Was it possible that God had placed them here, together? To help one another through this?

"You're missing your wilderness friends about now, I imagine."

Cassie looked at him in surprise. "As a matter of fact, not at all. I miss the easier terrain of the Appalachian Trail, but now that we've made it here, to the top, all we need to do is follow the water, right? The fjord takes us to Base Camp. We'll make it, Daniel!"

A strong gust of wind he'd estimate had to be near gale strength seemed to come out of nowhere and she rocked on her heels, buffeted like a nylon pennant. He grabbed her upper arm.

"Hang on!" Scouring the landscape, his searching gaze caught on several rock outcroppings, all covered in thick moss, with sparse trees growing between them. He pointed, unable to fight both the wind and his rib cage by speaking. Cassie nodded, they wrapped arms around each other's waist, stepped out heads down and aimed for the safe spot.

He could tell Cassie was worried about his injuries as she clutched his jacket and not him. Gratitude filled him with more of that warm sensation. He was glad Cassie was at his side. Not because he wanted to protect her, which he definitely did. It was a natural reflex with her. No, Daniel was happy because he'd never felt so calm, so in-the-moment, as he did with her. They were a good pair.

Careful, buddy. You almost thought "couple."

Fear clutched at his joy vibes, working to tear them apart. It was one thing to battle the elements. But to battle his heart, to risk being hurt by a woman again?

It was nothing less than terrifying.

Cassie wanted to ignore how easily she fit in the nook of Daniel's arm, how safe and secure a place it was beside him. But other than having his ribs to focus on, which she took care not to squeeze or bump, she couldn't think about anything besides this very moment. The wind was relentless from all sides, and if she'd been alone she was certain she'd not be able to move as quickly. She'd probably have dropped to her knees to avoid being blown over and crawled to what looked like a good campsite.

Instead, they faced this latest challenge together. Definitely something she could get used to, but knew she shouldn't. Daniel wasn't interested in any kind of romantic entanglement, hadn't he made that clear?

People change their minds.

"Here." She felt more than heard Daniel's declaration

as the wind was so loud and talking was impossible. They trekked to the leeward side of the rock formation, and leaned against the wall, the immediate silence as unsettling as the surprise gust of wind had been.

"That was extreme." She pulled her hood off, suddenly warmer than she'd been all day. "Out of the gusts it's so much warmer."

"We'll make camp here. I'll handle the fire if you can get some wood. Maybe try over there?" He pointed to several clumps of leafless bushes. "If the wind gets to you, lie flat."

Cassie didn't need her intuition to tell her Daniel was hurting. No way would he encourage her to risk going back into the wind without him by her side if he wasn't. Instead of confronting him, though, she decided getting their fire going was the top priority. She could try to get him to admit how much he was hurting later, by the warmth of the flames.

The wind didn't let up but she kept as low a profile as possible, cutting at the branches with Daniel's survival knife. It made her blade, a new purchase she'd packed as a precaution against wildlife or having to cut rappel lines quickly, look like a nail file. It took her a matter of seconds to gather enough wood to get the fire started. When she returned to the protected area, Daniel was already making his igniter spark against kindling he'd shoved in his pack this morning.

They spent the last hour of daylight setting up his tarp, using the rocks as one wall of their tiny fortress, and their packs as weights on corners of the nylon fabric. The air was relatively still behind the rocks, blocking the sunset glimpsed as she walked back with the firewood.

Daniel actually relented and let her boil the water for their MREs. Finally, the man was seeing common sense.

"This is tastier than last night's." She licked her lips of the remaining chicken stew, wondering if she'd have a protein bar or pack of almonds for dessert. "I'm glad we refilled at the lake." There were three bottles of water left; they'd filled empty bottles they'd carried in from the tiny airport, and they each had a larger bottle they'd packed.

"I've never had a meal under the stars that wasn't delicious." Daniel's low voice was almost back to normal, with only a small but detectable roughness on the edges.

"How badly are you hurting, Daniel?"

"I'm good. Honest. I thought I might have cracked a few ribs, but they must be only bruised. The pain isn't so bad when I'm still, or not trying to go so fast while climbing up and out of a mountain pass."

She couldn't stop the laughter that rolled so easily around him. "You are the only person I know who can make the hardest things in life seem like a cake walk."

"Glad you're amused." He took a small sip of the water.

"Are you worried we'll run out of water?"

"Not at all. You saw the fjord. We're following it the rest of the way out. It'll be good for us until we reach the Labradorimiut settlement, Way Point. I have to warn you, it's not even a real settlement, thus the name. It's more of a launch pad for researchers and the like."

"Wait—you don't think we'll be rescued before

then?" She'd memorized his map and the tiny village-like spot he'd highlighted had to be several days away by foot.

His gaze met hers over the fire, the stress of their ordeal plainly etched in the lines between his nose and mouth, and between his brows. "We can't count on it, Cassie. I'll keep trying my sat phone, but the likelihood of catching a signal isn't great enough to depend on."

"Oh." Was that her voice, so whiny? She cleared her throat. "I mean, okay. We're going to do whatever it takes."

But as night and the temperatures fell, so did the optimism that had always come naturally to her. It was foolish to think that just because they'd survived so much already, they'd make it the rest of the way without issue.

A plaintive howl pierced the constant pitch of the wind, sending shivers over her shoulders, her nape and down her back. She was on her feet, Daniel's knife back in her hand before she had a chance to rethink.

"Hang on, Cassie. It's okay. Look." Daniel turned on his small flashlight and swept it across the land, the rays of illumination spilling out at least one hundred feet. It took her a bit but on his third sweep she saw them—bright spots, in pairs, aimed at them. Upon closer inspection, she could see the sun's remaining rays reflected in their eyes.

"Wolves?" She'd never seen them anywhere but a wolf preserve in Pennsylvania.

"Coyotes, most likely. Hard to tell from this far in the dim light." He flicked his flashlight off.

"What if they're wolves?"

"We're safe. Chances are they won't approach the fire. If they do, I have the rifle. You take charge of the flares and bear spray."

"Wow, I'm honored. You trust me with the bear spray?" She tried to keep it light, playful. Daniel had the world on his shoulders with always thinking ahead of their situation, knowing the perfect way to handle each obstacle. The last thing he needed was to be concerned about her turning into a flake because of her own exhaustion and stress.

"Have I given you any reason to think you'd have to use it on me?" His tone was equally jovial but the thread of hurt in it made her want to weep.

"No, not at all, not for one minute. I'm sorry, Daniel. I was trying to let you know you don't have to worry about me. I know I've freaked out a few times, but honestly, I can handle whatever I need to."

"Are you kidding me, Cassie? You are the bravest woman I know."

Chapter Ten

Daniel's comment reached into her heart and before she could try to stop them tears rolled down her cheeks.

"Hey, that was supposed to be a compliment."

"I know. I have no idea why I'm so weepy." She swiped at her cheeks, myriad emotions spinning together—joy, relief, affection—into the solid thread she suspected had been forming between her and Daniel since they'd stepped aboard their tragic flight.

His hand rubbed in between her shoulders, the comfort real and visceral. "You've been through a lot, Cassie. We both have. If you need a cry, do it. I know I was ready to sob when we were on the path."

"When I slipped over?"

"Yes."

"But you didn't. You saved my life."

"I had something to focus on, is all. Trust me, you'll see me shed some tears before the end of our time here, I'm sure. We're being pushed to our limits."

She nodded, sipped some of her remaining water. "This isn't how I expected this to go, not at all." A giggle brewed and burst forth at the ludicrousness of her words. Daniel joined her in what for her was a deep belly laugh, but she noticed his laughs were a little lighter. Shallower.

"Oh, Daniel, I'm so sorry. The last thing you need is to laugh with your ribs hurting."

"It's worth it." His smile was more of a grimace and she had to bite the inside of her cheeks to keep from dissolving into more laughter. Leave it to her nervous habit of giggling to run roughshod over an intimate moment of heartfelt sharing.

"I have faith that someday we'll tell this story and see a lot more humor in it, while honoring Sean's memory without the sting of losing him like we did." She spoke to the fire, not trusting herself to keep from grinning inappropriately if she looked directly at Daniel. They'd lost Sean on this trip and she didn't intend to take from the gravity of his death. Something about Daniel had helped lift the cloud of grief from her soul, made her know that one day she'd be happy again. Would another man have done the same?

Her conscience kept nudging her. There was a chance that she and Daniel were looking for the same thing, the same crash site. Why was she holding back from confronting him about it?

Maybe you don't want to ruin what seems to be a good thing growing between you.

Considering they were in the midst of a fight to stay alive, she knew this was a significant revelation. But not one she was willing to entertain. Not after being so hurt by the man she last dated.

Daniel remained quiet and after another moment she

risked a peek. His profile, now as familiar as her own, was stark and pensive, his face illuminated with flickering flames of light. Realization dawned. Did he think she meant *we* as in she thought they were more than two stranded hikers, forced together because of lethal circumstances?

"Daniel, I didn't mean *we* as anything serious, I mean…and I am not for one minute forgetting about Sean—"

"Stop." He reached over and grasped her hand. "It's okay, whatever you've thought, because I've thought it, too."

They both had gloves off as the fire's warmth was pretty intense. His skin was warm, his hands strong. As they sat, still, staring into the fire, she let herself relax and enjoy the moment. She was beginning to get drowsy when another howl cut through the night.

"It's okay." He gave her hand a quick squeeze, then let go. The fire didn't feel as hot and she groped for her gloves in the absence of Daniel's touch. "That's how they communicate, is all. We're safe, Cassie. We'll keep the fire going all night, and they'll leave us alone. Why don't you get ready to take the first shift? I'll use the facilities and try to get some rest."

"As long as you leave the flare gun handy, I'm good with that."

As he slowly made his way around the outcropping, Cassie unrolled and then folded her bedroll into a comfortable cushion. Her bones ached and the skin on her face felt crocodile skin–dry but none of it bothered her the way she knew it would if she had only herself to worry about. Being concerned for Daniel seemed to give her a purpose, something that kept her from deadly anxiety. The kind where existential thoughts could run amok.

Existential or possible?

She poked at the fire with a stick, wishing they had more water. A hot cup of tea would heat her from the inside. Her tea bags, so carefully packed and in the bottom of her backpack, were useless until they found a new fresh water source. No way was she wasting precious drinking liquid on a caffeinated beverage.

The coyotes' howls reached through the dark, across the fire, and she grabbed the can of bear spray from the pile of provisions Sean had left in his go bag. Poor Sean, unable to see how much he had helped them. The crunch of footsteps signaled Daniel's return, breaking her from the beginning of a trip down melancholy lane. She stood, ready to take her turn.

"Hang on, Cassie." His gaze searched hers. "I've been thinking." The laser intensity of his statement made it feel like snowflakes were flicking against the inside of her stomach.

"About?"

"If my map's right, and that is Nachvak Fjord, we have a real shot at reaching the wreck. Without putting ourselves at extra risk. Or, rather, more risk than we're already going to face."

"The B-17? You mean we could see it, be right there?" Hope flared at being able to tell her family she'd stood at Eugenia's final resting place, then quickly died as she processed what he said. "It'll take us out of range for a rescue, right?" With Daniel injured, possibly worse than he was admitting, it wouldn't be worth the risk.

No matter how much each of them longed to see what remained of the Flying Fortress. Staying alive was top priority.

He nodded. "You realize you were never going to get anywhere close to it with your assigned tour group, don't you? The tourist jaunts from Base Camp don't come out this far. By my estimates we're no more than twenty miles from it."

She was surprised there was one iota of a struggle inside her about what to do. How easy it was to dismiss the almost-dying parts of her trip here.

"No, absolutely not. It's not worth it if it means we could end up perishing out here, Daniel."

"Think about it, Cassie. It's the entire reason you've come. We've got time before winter really moves in or prevents us from leaving Base Camp."

"We're already going to be a week off our schedules, and that's if we get to Base Camp in what? Three more days? More?"

"Hey, I don't want to mess with your focus. I get it. But I had to put the offer out here for us to discuss. At most it would add two days to our trip back to Base Camp." Daniel's forthrightness was evident, but she wondered if he had a motive he didn't want to share.

"Wait—why exactly do you want to try to find it?" She paused. It had to be a good reason if he was willing to put up with his aching ribs that much longer. "Is how much you earn based upon whether or not you find the wreck?" She'd never asked him, she'd been so self-involved about her own survival, her heart's desire to at least get near the B-17.

"I'd like to try to see if we can go by it. It's not about

the money, not totally." He held up his hands, palms up. "Yes, I get a significant bonus if I find the, er, wreck." He stopped talking and his mouth turned into a thin line. There was something else he wasn't saying but her bladder wasn't offering her the time to ask him more.

"Let me pray on it tonight, Daniel. Right now, all I can think about is taking care of nature. Mind if I take this with me?" She held up the can of bear spray. Daniel laughed.

"Not at all. I had this with me, you know." He swung the rifle off his back, his pained grunt making her ribs hurt in empathy.

"Now's a good time to take that NSAID. While your belly's still full." She normally wasn't about telling anyone what to do, but keeping each other's health and well-being a priority was both of their responsibilities, at least until they were rescued.

"Thanks for the reminder."

She walked beyond their site only as far as she absolutely needed to for privacy. The close bond she'd formed with Daniel was another thing she'd be afraid of, if there wasn't already enough with moose, wolves, bears and cliffs. She'd never allowed herself to depend on a man before. It was important to Cassie to be as self-sufficient as possible when out in nature. Just in case her hiking partner was injured or didn't show up. Sure, they were stranded and had to rely on each other as much as possible. But in her heart, new chords were striking emotions and a sense of attachment she only associated with him.

Take Daniel's injured ribs. It struck fear into her not only because she was concerned about his well-being, but because she'd developed a new fear she'd never had before. Fear of losing Daniel. Which was ridiculous, because she didn't *have* Daniel. He wasn't hers.

Before her heart started racing from anxiety over all the things she couldn't control, she finished up and got back to camp. They had a long day ahead of them tomorrow.

Daniel used the time Cassie was taking care of nature to try to justify holding back the real reason he wanted, *needed*, to check out the B-17. He couldn't do it, though. There was no reason for him to not tell her about the possibility of the treasure that may or may not have been on the same B-17 her great-grandmother had flown. The private jewelry box of Catherine the Great, secreted out of Saint Petersburg—then Leningrad—Russia, to England, and then far away from Nazi possession. The box and its valuable contents were believed to have been on Great-grandma Eugenia's flight. Several jewelry pieces gifted to the Empress could be in the box.

Daniel reminded himself that the odds of the treasure remaining with the wreck after all this time, even in such a remote location, were close to nil. Which was why his employer, while paying him handsomely to search for the wreck and covering all travel expenses, wasn't going to hand Daniel the top limit of the contract unless he found the treasure and saw that it was turned over to the local government. The hope was that the jewels would return to Russia, for museum display.

Daniel loved that he was able to both contribute to history by helping treasures return to their rightful owners, often an entire nation. He wouldn't accept a contract that didn't spell this out. But he'd be lying to himself if he didn't recognize the tug in his gut for what it was. Excitement that the funds for the land he wanted to purchase could really happen.

But more and more he was developing a loyalty to Cassie and her needs. He didn't want to disappoint her in any way, and what faster way to lose someone's respect and trust was there than lying?

It wasn't lying, not really. *Yes, it is.* His thoughts played tug-of-war with his conscience and his stomach didn't feel so great, his MRE refusing to settle and be digested.

Forgive me. Show me what to do, God.

Cassie's soft footfalls, followed by the warmth of her nearness as she sat on her folded bed roll, added to his increasing belief that he owed her more than he would a stranger or fellow treasure hunter. They searched for the same wreckage, but each for their own valuable reasons. He wanted to right history's wrongs and provide a wonderful opportunity for his students. Cassie wanted to bring peace to her grandmother's remaining days.

"You're supposed to be sleeping," she chided him as she took the rifle from his grasp and lay it across her lap. "What do you always tell me? 'You're sleeping for both of us.'"

He chuckled. "I didn't think you paid that much attention to what I say."

"You mean I don't look like I'm hanging on to each and every word?" She smiled and it warmed her expression ten times more than the firelight.

"You don't need me to tell you what to do. You would have managed on your own, you know."

"That's a bunch of hooey."

"No, it's not. You were packed to survive two weeks without another food source, and so far we haven't come across any wildlife that you couldn't manage on your own."

"Um, you're forgetting one thing. I almost fell to my early demise."

"If you hadn't been talking to me, you wouldn't have had reason to turn around and slip in the first place."

"Daniel, I hate to break it to you, but if it had been up to me, I never would have left the lake. I'd have waited for a search and rescue to find me, hoping and praying they'd followed Sean's flight plan."

Her words stabbed deep into the conscience he'd already scoured for faults. He rubbed his sternum, careful not to move his ribs. "Uh, I need to tell you something."

Sharp, laser-blue eyes searched his. He saw the moment her trust faded, then retreated. It was as if a glacier had moved over his soul. "What's that?"

"I asked Sean to deviate from the flight pattern he filed. Not by a lot, but, well, enough."

"What are you talking about?" He hated how still she sat, the warmth he'd gotten used to shut behind her defenses.

"I wanted to see if we could fly over where I think the wreck is."

"And did we?"

"No. As I've mentioned, it's between us and Base Camp. But the reality is that we're not going to have a search and rescue come after us, not until we're another two days closer to our destination. We're too far out of satellite range to send our location. We crashed almost one hundred miles southwest of Base Camp."

Cassie's gaze left his and it was worse than having her glare focused on him. "You said eighty miles, and that it was a straight shot. Now's a fine time to tell me we have another twenty miles, probably two days, to go."

"I was afraid you'd lose hope. We had a long way to go to get off the mountain. Besides, I didn't know exactly, not yet. I'd hoped my estimate was wrong. I'm sorry, Cassie."

"I'm not happy that you misled me in any way, Daniel. For what it's worth, I forgive you. We're in an incredible situation—you did your best in the moment. As I'm doing, with the information I have right now. I've made up my mind. I want to find the B-17 if we can. It's this close to us, on the way to Base Camp with just a little deviation." She looked at the map, intent as her finger traced a line between where they sat, Base Camp, and where he figured the wreck lay. "I vote to go for it. I never expected this chance, to be so close, much less see it. I thought I'd be paying my respects to an entire geographical area. Now, I might actually be able to send Grandma Rose a photo of her mother's resting place." She folded the map, handed it back to him. "You waited too long, but thank you for sharing the truth with me after all. I get that you had your reasons. Please understand that I have mine for insisting we're going to do whatever we have to, to get to Eugenia's plane." And that was it. Cassie turned away and looked into the distance as if he wasn't there.

Her silence hurt more than angry words or accusations ever could. After several minutes, she turned back to face him. "You really need to get some rest, Daniel. I've got it for now."

"Not until we settle this. I really messed up, Cassie."

"Yeah, you did." Cold puffs of breath left her mouth and she didn't make eye contact.

He lay down, the heat of the fire combined with his sleeping bag enough to allow him to relax despite the freezing temperatures. The wind hadn't abated and the cold edge to it foretold colder weather, most likely a storm. He opened his mouth to tell Cassie his concerns, but thought better of it. He'd ruined her night enough as it was.

The least he could do was allow her to realize that he wasn't the great man or rescuer he feared she saw him as. It was for the best, because nothing could come from anything they felt growing between them. She'd made it clear she wasn't looking for a man; she'd been hurt too deeply and too recently.

His logic warred with the loss he experienced as a deep grief. As if by admitting to Cassie he was to blame for them not being saved yet, he'd forfeited any right to her friendship, much less her trust. He knew it was for the best that neither of them had any illusion that their partnership was for anything more than survival.

But if he was so certain about what was best, why did he feel like he wanted to howl like the wolves and coyotes they'd run across?

Chapter Eleven

Cassie took it as a good sign that her footsteps felt more solid with each mile since they'd broken camp this morning. They had two solid days of hiking behind them since the first night after her almost-plummet to certain death off the side of the mountain. Since Daniel had admitted that he thought it was his fault they hadn't been rescued yet. It had jarred her out of the feelings she'd thought were growing between them. Until she realized that the feelings weren't gone. They were deeper. Daniel's ability to admit his wrong and ask her forgiveness had only strengthened her respect for him, no matter how irritated she'd been.

She'd tossed and turned that whole night after his revelation, unable to take advantage of her rest periods. Only after she'd prayed and asked God to help her figure it all out had she fallen into a brief but deep slumber. Yet several days out she was still feeling the lack of sleep; the long, long hours of constant physical exertion had worn her down. And she was still in one piece, unlike Daniel, whom she grew more certain each mile had fractured his ribs.

It would have been a shorter journey to the shores of the fjord if Daniel hadn't been injured, if her bones and muscles still weren't so achy from the crash. They were both relying on their mutual supply of anti-inflammatory medications, as a hot bath wasn't an option. The thought alone of her apartment tub, filled with hot steaming water and scented bath salts, was near torture. She put thoughts of what-could-have-been out of her mind and concentrated on each step, her footprints falling alongside Daniel's; she'd insisted he take the lead each day since he'd saved her life for the second time.

The only answer she'd discerned from her prayer time was to practice forgiveness. And yet, she wasn't sure Daniel had anything to be forgiven for, not by her. Sure, he'd had Sean take them away from their original flight plan, but it wasn't his fault they'd hit that weather. What hurt her most was that he hadn't told her his concerns. She'd felt like his true partner, a trusted friend and yes, confidante. Finding out he'd held something back crushed her.

Your ego's bruised.

It was true, and she needed to clear the air with him, but there hadn't been a right time to approach him and tell him how she felt. They were on a tight schedule to make it to Way Point.

And she'd told him the truth—she wanted to see where Great-grandma Eugenia had perished. It was worth it, after all they'd been through. The more she thought about it, the more it seemed that it might be a blessing that they'd crashed where they had. She didn't for one minute believe that God meant for them to crash, or for Sean to die, but Cassie knew in her heart that faith and prayer opened the door for God to bring good out of the direst situations.

Despite what had to be at times excruciating pain, Daniel steadfastly continued forward, carrying his pack and the rifle. She'd stuffed as much of Sean's provisions as possible into her pack, and even though it weighed twice as much as she'd ever carried in Pennsylvania, it was manageable.

The only thing that wasn't positive as far as she was concerned were the big fat snowflakes that had been falling in a lacey curtain since breakfast. There was no telling if Sean's distress signal had been received, and they still hadn't come upon cellular coverage. But the old-fashioned compass worked fine, and they were able to conserve the batteries on their phones, where they'd each downloaded maps, thanks to Daniel's hardcopy maps. They would reach Way Point sometime tomorrow.

Daniel's forward motion stopped abruptly and she almost banged into him, her nose no more than an inch from his pack.

"What is it?" she whispered, used to these unexpected stops as they came across various wildlife. Thankfully, so far they'd only seen more moose, elk and a small herd of caribou earlier today. All far enough away to observe without the roaring fear of that first moose encounter.

He held up his right hand, fisted, instead of making a sound. Cassie knew it meant to be still, silent. Her heart sounded in her ears and she was positive anything nearby could hear it, too. A rushing noise.

Daniel unfolded his map. "Here." His finger pointed to a spot very close to his X, where she knew he thought the B-17 was. "That's the waterfall that's here." He moved his finger, showing her the direct route.

"We're that close?" Wonder made each breath seem frozen in time. The snowfall surrounded them, and it was easy to believe it was December in Pennsylvania and not August in the Torngat Mountains.

He looked around, turning a full 360 degrees as he did so. There wasn't any danger of a sudden drop-off as they were close to, if not right at, sea level. Fjord level, as she'd started to think of it. "I think it's possible your great-grandmother flew in along the fjord as her visual, then crashed somewhere along here. We've found other wrecks that historians believe met the same fate."

"It's not hard to imagine her getting into trouble with this kind of weather in the summer. And they didn't have all of the navigation equipment we do." Not to mention GPS.

"No, they didn't. There's so much capability in our cell phones, too. If we could have saved the helicopter, the radio alone would have been a huge help."

She didn't want to chat away the rest of their daylight talking about things they already knew. "Let's find it, Daniel."

"I'm working on it." He smiled, but it wasn't the wide grin he'd offered days ago. Before he'd admitted he hadn't told her everything about his conversation with Sean.

They came upon the waterfall within minutes, and

Cassie wasted no time slipping off her backpack and taking out her water containers. "This is a gift!" She'd thought she'd done great, managing their water as they found it. Two nights ago they'd camped by a small creek, probably no more than a trickle by this terrain's standards. But it had been enough to sustain them through today.

Daniel followed suit. "I figured we'd have the fjord if we never found these falls but this works." They spent the next several minutes filling their bottles and drinking the cold, clean liquid.

"No specialty beverage will ever taste as good as this does." Cassie had slowed her guzzle to sips, grateful for a chance to quench her thirst.

Daniel capped his second large bottle. "We need to keep moving, Cassie. I don't think the wreckage is far from here, if it's survived the elements."

The concern in his expression tugged at her compassion but she held back. She was still emotionally raw from finding out that he'd kept all of what he'd known about their possibility of rescue to himself for so long. Plus what if there was something of value to her, to Grandma Rose, at the site? An artifact that Daniel believed it was his right to claim for his employer? Would she have the courage, the fortitude, to claim anything that had been Eugenia's?

It's not about any material "thing."

She knew this. It was about representing her family, giving Grandma Rose much deserved peace of mind that they'd never given up on Eugenia and in fact, were paying her homage in the best possible way.

"It's really damp for something that can rust, isn't it?"

"Yes." He didn't elaborate but instead struck out to the north, map in hand. Cassie followed, but instead of keeping her focus centered on his steps or back, she swept her gaze over the landscape. It'd be so easy to miss a decayed piece of metal among the myriad trees and ground shrubs. Unlike at the top of the mountain, the vegetation here was thicker and dense. She knew the snowfall had to be significant to make it all the way to ground level, and the dusting down here was indicative of several inches at higher altitude.

Plus it meant that even if a rescue flight knew about them, it'd be next to impossible to find or save them. Not during a storm. Stomping her feet, she fought off her fear of an impending storm. It was the fog, the exhaustion. No matter what, she'd committed to the risk. All to bring healthy closure for Grandma Rose.

They were almost a half hour from the waterfall when she saw something that didn't match the rest of the forest floor. A single arc of snow, coating what could be a wayward branch, but she'd never seen a tree limb shaped like the tail of a World War II bomber.

"Daniel!"

But he must have spied it, too, as he was moving across the ground to the east, his strides careful, his expression eager. Anticipation swirled in her belly and she rushed to keep up with him. What seemed easy hiking turned into slow plods as they had to lift their knees higher to clear the underbrush. The space between the trees narrowed, and Daniel turned to face her.

"We have to take our packs off and squeeze through these. We'll come back for them."

"Sure thing."

They eased themselves through, until there was a sudden clearing. From where she and Daniel stood, Cassie saw that the trees surrounding what appeared to be an airplane, or at least half of it, were thinner in the trunk than those of the forest they'd hiked through the last two days.

"It's as if all of the trees were wiped out." Her breath formed puffs of condensation and she wiped the large snowflakes from her lashes, her cheeks. "Do you, is it…" She was afraid to ask, fearful that this was indeed a dream and not answer to two generations of prayer.

"The tail is definitely vintage. We need to see the cockpit and the fuselage to make a certain identification, but I can tell you this is a B-17 tail. I've seen a lot in my travels." He spoke reverently, as if he'd uncovered the Holy Grail. She imagined that a find like this was special for a historian like Daniel.

"What are we waiting for? Let's check the rest of it out."

"First, no walking or climbing on top of it, and we need to do our best to not step on anything that could be the last remnants of it, like the wings. It's remarkable that this much has survived." He carefully moved the snow off the large steel piece that he'd identified as the tail. Too excited to simply watch, Cassie stepped next to him and helped. They were like kids making snow angels, using their gloved hands to swipe away the flakes, similar to windshield wipers.

The image of an eagle screaming down from the sky appeared under their hands. Cassie's knees began to shake, her stomach flipped.

"Daniel. It's the squadron logo for Eugenia's unit."

Her voice trembled and tears flowed. She didn't care how she looked, or if she seemed overly sentimental. This was the find of a lifetime, three lifetimes, three generations of her family.

"Yes, yes, it is." He stopped and stared at an area of the fuselage he'd cleared of snow, dirt and leaves. "See the numbers under here?" Faded numbers and letters were stenciled under the squadron logo.

She nodded. "That's a call sign. It matches the logbook I found online, in the war archives. It also includes all but the first two numbers of the aircraft serial number." She'd cross-referenced army, air force, and multiple museum records with what her family knew about Eugenia's squadron and her dates of active service.

"Did you get access to the unit history or aircraft logbook?" Daniel's query wasn't accusatory but genuinely curious.

"No, but I'm pretty certain we're looking at Eugenia's B-17. We're in the right locale. It's a B-17, right? And it has her squadron's symbol. What more do I really need?" The days and nights of constant vigilance against the elements and wildlife weighed in on her, and she wasn't able to think with any semblance of calm. "I have to believe it's hers."

"We need the serial number of the aircraft to verify. At least, for my employer I need the exact serial number, and photos of it. But yes, I do think it's your great-grandmother's plane."

She studied him. "You have the numbers, don't you? Why didn't you tell me?"

"I have serial numbers for several different aircraft that disappeared in this region, during World War II and after." He looked away, and it was as if he was shy, unable to meet her gaze. "I wanted the discovery to be yours. Your family's."

Daniel's considerate, generous gesture that had her heartbeat racing, an overwhelming urge to hug him, made her arms shake all the more. It was impossible to see him as a man who'd deliberately kept information about their flight and location from her, no matter how badly he felt. Daniel's heart was pure, his motives in the right place.

Cassie waited for him to meet her gaze again, enjoyed the immediate connection that flared when it did. "That's the nicest thing anyone's done for me in a long while. Maybe ever." He hadn't been hiding it from her but keeping it as a surprise, a gift, for her and her family. She blinked, holding back the tears of gratitude that fought to fall. This was not the time to go all emotional. She didn't want to miss one detail of the B-17. "Tell me about the serial numbers."

Daniel had to admit, it was gratifying to be able to confirm for Cassie that this bird had been flown by her great-grandmother. He wasn't certain when it had happened, but Cassie's success was bound with his. His happiness had everything to do with her happiness, as well as her family's joy when they eventually found out, as if Eugenia and Rose were his relatives, too.

Since he and Cassie had confirmed the call number on the tail with the serial number he had that matched a B-17 that never made it back from the UK in the middle of the war, they'd agreed to use the rest of their day to explore and see if there was anything worth finding in the wreck. They'd been working against the constant heavy, wet snowfall and his muscles were about to call it a day. Not to mention his ribs, which limited how high he could reach. As for pulling branches and brush away from the wreck? Forget it. He'd need a team of researchers with the right equipment to make a dent in what now was little more than the frame of an aircraft, filled with decades of dirt, snow, ice and water.

"We've been looking for the last—" Cassie looked at her watch "—three hours." She swiped an errant hair from her brow, revealing the lines on her forehead that indicated her disappointment. "I was certain we'd have found something, anything, by now."

"It's how it goes with this kind of exploration."

"I know, but to be this close…" She kicked at the ground, hands on hips, catching her breath. "You're not going to get your full paycheck if you can't see the serial number, and there's no way to get to the nose and cabin. Not in this weather, maybe not at all."

"It's okay. I found the plane." It was true. Sure, the extra bonus to have found the treasure from Europe would have been wonderful, but not mandatory. Not anymore. Being alive, saving Cassie—these had become higher priorities.

"You got me here, in more ways than one. I want to be able to do something nice for you."

Fear gripped him. There she went again, singing his praises. Daniel couldn't handle her words, not when he'd begun this trip with one goal: find the treasure. The fact that Cassie had become important to him didn't excuse how focused on that he'd been.

"Cassie, before you think I only kept the part about

asking Sean to fly over the wreck, out of our way, from you, I need to say something else."

She tilted her head. "You're a government agent and now you have to kill me?" Her deadpan delivery was priceless.

"No, nothing that glamorous. I'm looking for a treasure believed to be with this plane. It's possible that Eugenia was carrying historically significant treasure with her, to save it from the Nazis. I'm not supposed to talk about it, due to an NDA, but I know I can trust you."

"I remember reading a snippet about that in the squadron's history. That wasn't uncommon at all, was it?"

"No."

"So why do you feel badly about not telling me?"

He blinked. "Because I never want to be anything less than one-hundred percent truthful with you." He'd never spoken truer words. And Cassie's willingness to forgive and forget was truly humbling.

"It's a detail for your job, Daniel. You've been so giving of your time and knowledge with me. Did I want to get stranded almost a hundred miles from Base Camp with a complete stranger? No, no way. But I did. We did. And I'm so glad it was you." A cloud of fear passed over her expression and it twisted his insides to think about the possibility of anyone else leading her out of their crash.

Life without Cassie was becoming something he hardly remembered.

It's the trauma you've been through talking, buddy.

He wasn't certain it was anything but the truth of how he and Cassie worked, hiked and survived together as if they'd known one another for years. They communicated just like his parents, as if they'd been together forever. Was there a chance he and Cassie could ever have what his parents, and his grandparents before them, shared?

"I can't explain why it bothers me, Cassie. I know that neither of us owed the other anything. We were passengers on the same ill-fated flight. As we've spent more time together, it's become easier to talk to you."

"And harder to hold things in." She grinned. "I get it."

Bam. His heart kicked into overdrive, as if acknowledging a gift from above. Her acceptance of his shortcomings blew him away. None of the other women he'd dated had ever been so kind.

Cassie was one of a kind. "You have every right to be upset that I cost us more time on the ground, and that I didn't tell you how much I had riding on finding the wreck and what could be inside it."

"Since you're being honest, I'm going to admit something to you. I wasn't thrilled to hear about your request to Sean. Nope, not at all. Just think—if you'd asked him in front of me, we'd have found out we were looking for the same plane, and we might have been able to help one another sooner. Or rather, you'd help me." She held up both hands, palms out in surrender. "You're the expert with the history, no question. And your acumen in the wilderness has saved both our lives ten times over."

"That's beside the point."

"No, it isn't. I'm not finished. I was most upset because it reminded me of how I was duped by Jim, that guy I met online. He'd led me to believe things were different than they were. I don't like feeling I've been patronized or kept out of the loop. But in truth, Daniel? Why you're here is none of my business. I mean it. So believe me when I say I'm not holding a grudge against you for anything. Speaking for myself, I've learned a lot about life over the past long days. I'm not the woman who crashed into the lake, not by a long shot. If you need to hear the words, then listen. I forgive you."

He wanted to be able to reply with something meaningful. Let Cassie know how much he respected her. But all he could do was stare at the most fearless, honest person he'd ever known.

"I talk too much." She slipped off her gloves. Daniel stared at the tail and the fuselage they'd tried to clear without any success. Yeah, the treasure might be inside there. And it was going to stay there. Nothing was more important than protecting Cassie.

Chapter Twelve

"We can't spend any more time exploring right now." Daniel's mouth was in the grim line Cassie recognized. He never said he was worried outright in the moment, but only after, once whatever danger they faced had passed. She took in their surroundings again, noting the steady snowfall. The tree canopy gave the illusion that it was a moderate storm. Yet all she needed to do was look back the way they'd come, out toward the fjord and its shores, and she saw nothing but a white wall.

"It's hard to be this close and unable to dig up anything more." Now that they'd identified the airframe as best as possible, and confirmed it was most likely the plane, Cassie wanted to focus all of her energy and time on seeing if there was anything Eugenia had left behind. It was sobering to consider that her great-grandmother perished on this spot, that her remains might be among the rusted-out parts of the plane that had become part of the forest floor. She knew from her research that she'd need to contact the United States Department of Defense, which had a special office that dealt with repatriating the remains of fallen service members. The WASPs hadn't received all the respect and consideration due them until the last couple of decades, but at this point there was no question Eugenia's remains, if found, would be treated with the utmost dignity and protocol.

"I'm as eager as you to see what else is here, Cassie, but the snow's not letting up. It's the storm we've had all the signs of." Indeed they had. The blustery winds when they'd first climbed atop the mountain, right after she'd almost fallen to her death. The bank of clouds on the western horizon the next day, followed by more wind. Then today's bad weather.

"I'm not arguing with you. We'll have tomorrow morning to look." She planned on using her flashlight to do some digging tonight. Sure, she'd need to get through the snow, but she'd been through too much to not give herself, and Eugenia, the chance to see what this wreck still held.

"We're hiking out tomorrow. It's not worth more time here."

"You've found the wreck you were hoping for, right? So you'll get a portion of that bonus check." She spoke as she walked toward him and reached for the tarp he had folded and put in the front pocket of his pack.

"Here, wait." He shrugged the pack off, unable to do so without biting his lower lip against the discomfort.

"You haven't taken another ibuprofen since this morning, have you?"

"I'm saving it for tonight. It's actually getting a bit better each day."

"Liar."

"Maybe."

They both laughed as they fell into their established routine.

"It's a lot easier to set this up with trees." She hooked bungee cord around one trunk, attached it to the tarp's corner metal grommet, then repeated with another corner. "I think we need the tarp to hang at an angle, do you agree? The weight of the snow could have it fall on us before morning."

"Definitely." He was breathing heavily, the exertion of clearing the snow from a large enough area to camp evident. Her constant companion, anxiety over Daniel's well-being, hopped onto her shoulder and began shouting in her ear.

He's going to puncture a lung. Maybe he already has. If anything happens to Daniel, you'll never make it out of here.

"No." She spoke quietly and firmly, not caring if Daniel thought she was losing it after so many days of life-threatening experiences.

"'No,' what?" His voice was equally low-pitched as he knelt on the ground and pulled his flint lighter from his pocket.

"When did you get that pile of twigs?" Had she been so focused on the tarp that she'd not noticed he'd walked off to gather wood?

More like you were worrying yourself silly over him.

"They're all over. Just covered by several inches of snow right now." He worked his tool, and the blue sparks quickly flew. But no smoke.

"The wood's too damp." Dread filled her. If they didn't have the warmth of the fire, they'd be okay. But the fire had been the one thing that kept the wild animals away at night. Now that they were in the forest, it wasn't hard to imagine that the likelihood of running into a bear might be higher.

"It'll start, don't stress." He kept at it.

"I'll try to find us more kindling, maybe some limbs." She tugged on the tarp to check that it was secure and made sure both their packs and all bags were under the protective cover. Cassie was grateful for space-age fabrics and technology. She knew that it wasn't very long ago that bringing a blanket or tarp on a long-haul hiking trip was a rare luxury. The ten-foot by ten-foot tarp she'd just set up had folded into a size not much larger than a deck of cards.

Cassie broke off a twig from low shrubs. It was a perfect broom to sweep away the snow and dead leaves from the ground around the aircraft. Her stomach flipped with anticipation. What would she do if she actually found a skeleton? It was against all odds that there would be any remains left after so long. Yet stories about World War II pilots whose remains were found decades after they crashed or were shot down weren't unheard of. As harsh as the climate was this far north, there was something to be said for its ability to preserve things. It was difficult to see much, as the day had faded to cotton ball fuzziness, so she pulled out her flashlight.

The beam caught on something she'd not expected; it appeared as if the wreck had become a part of the forest. Branches poked from all available openings, including the main cabin door. She stood on tiptoe, hoping to see more. The sight of snow inside the airframe deflated her eager anticipation. No matter how well preserved the aircraft looked under a coating of snow, there was no escaping that it had endured nearly eighty years with zero protection from the elements. Her vision blurred and she wanted to stomp her feet, yell at the airframe that at one time had been flown by her great-grandmother. Logic had repeatedly hinted that there was close to zip chance of her finding the wreck. Why couldn't she be happy, grateful, that at least they'd come upon it? That the awful circumstances that threatened her and Daniel's lives had at least allowed for this one grace?

"Not what you were expecting?" Daniel stood next to her and she couldn't look at him. Not until she got her emotions under control. Which seemed impossible as tears streamed through the snow that was freezing on her face. She shook her head.

"Hey, come here." He lay a hand on her shoulder and Cassie didn't need any further prompting as she turned into him and accepted his hug.

"Don't hurt your ribs." She sniffled against his jacket, the fasteners rubbing the tender skin on the tip of her nose.

"I'm fine, honest. Give yourself a minute. It's never as good or as bad as it seems."

She looked up at him, ready to see his smile. Instead, his dark eyes were somber, full of compassion. "Is that something you thought up on your own?"

"No. That's from my grandpa. He's always telling me to take it easy, not be in such a hurry to get wherever I think I need to be going." Daniel's expression grew thoughtful as he looked over her head toward the wreck. "He likes to hear about my summer adventures, but he thinks I'm working too hard to make the extra money I need to meet my goals. Says there's more to life than money."

"You're a high school teacher. I know it's not a Wall Street salary, but it can't be that bad."

"It's not, but I do have school loans. I earned my graduate degree a few years ago, too, so that added to my undergrad debt. But I didn't start doing these contracts to pay off my loans so much as to do something more hands-on with history."

"And get paid?"

He nodded. "Sure." He hesitated, as if weighing whether or not to tell her something. "The thing is, I have an idea of buying a nice plot of land in Western PA, to start my own survival hiking and exploring camp of sorts. History never dies, and I want to help keep it alive in some small way. By teaching other hikers what to look for, there's almost countless wrecks and historical landmarks waiting to be discovered."

"Daniel, that's exactly what I'm doing here, why I risked this kind of travel. I want to preserve my family history in the best way. I'm super interested in genealogy and our family tree. But history's not singular, is it? When I began looking up Eugenia's flight information, I saw that there are many other aircraft unaccounted for." Excitement filled her. She and Daniel had compared notes and were each searching for the same call sign. The same aircraft.

"Right, and World War II, while of special interest lately due to the seventy-fifth anniversary of the end of the war, is but one slice of history. Many other planes went down that we'll never find."

"So there's still a chance this isn't her aircraft, after all?"

"No, I have little doubt you're looking at her B-17. The odds are great, when you combine what your family history tells you with the historical facts staring us in the face here."

"But I need to verify this particular aircraft's serial number to be absolutely certain, right?"

"Yeah. And we can't look for it now."

"You're worried we won't make Base Camp before it closes for the season, aren't you?" The five weeks it was open a year were always the limiting factor for tourism to the area. She wished she'd planned to leave earlier in the summer instead of midway through.

"It's a definite concern." He said it as if they were discussing something mundane but she knew him well enough by now. Daniel was worried.

Daniel watched Cassie sleep, her face to the fire, or at least the tiny sliver of her face that wasn't covered by the sleeping bag or her wool cap. It was taking almost all their energy as they took turns to keep the flames going, as the driving wind and steady snowfall hadn't let up. He knew it'd all melt in a matter of hours in the sunlight, most likely, but surviving the night, the storm, was his priority right now. They'd changed their clothing again and were down to zero dry layers. Their base layer tops and bottoms were hanging close enough to the fire to dry, but with snow blowing under and around them, he worried they'd still be damp in the morning.

Morning. Only three more hours until full daylight, a chance to break through the snow and cloud cover with more light. It may as well be an eternity. Thoughts of hikers who'd never come back taunted him, made him second-guess every single action he'd encouraged them to take since the crash.

Since you asked Sean to veer off the standard, more direct, flight plan.

Cassie had forgiven him, so why couldn't he forgive himself? His mind scrambled for something positive to hang on to, anything but the reality he and Cassie faced.

Pray.

It wasn't unusual to find his mother hunkered with her first morning cup of coffee and her Bible, out on the back deck he'd helped his father build a few years back. Their suburban Pittsburgh property backed up to woods and Mom said she found her greatest peace during her "God time." She and his father never judged him for declining to join them at church service, and it had been easy to let the churchgoing go as he'd gone to college, moved out on his own and settled into his bachelor lifestyle.

Now, however, he longed for the Bible verses that he'd memorized each summer during Vacation Bible School. He needed something to grasp, as the constant howl of the storm was exhausting his adrenal glands. The cold and damp were the absolute pits, and none of it was helping his achy ribs. He hadn't lied to Cassie; the more he walked and got his blood flowing, the less his bones hurt. But when he had to sit still like this, or try to lie down, it was rough. His ability to take a deep breath was hindered but he'd had so many sports injuries over the years he was pretty sure he knew the difference between a cracked or bruised rib. And yet, he'd had to face his own powerlessness more than once this trip. Maybe he was wrong and he did have a fractured rib or two. But there was nothing he could do about it, not out here. Not until they reached some kind of civilization.

I can do all things through Him that strengthens me.

The words came to him unbidden, save for his strong desire to find an anchor in his current chaotic mental state. They might not be exact, but he recognized the meaning, the promise, of the verse from Philippians. It had been his mainstay when he'd wrestled in high school, and when he'd played intramural flag football in college. A naturally slender man, he'd never had the muscles that so many of his classmates took for granted. So he'd relied on a bigger power, something greater than himself. It could be the fatigue, the worry, but in that instant Daniel knew that it was time to make a big change in his life. When he got back to PA, he was going to find a local church ASAP. Or even go back to the one he'd grown up in; his parents lived only twenty minutes from him. What was a bit of a drive on Sunday mornings after so many days in the wilderness?

The thought made him chuckle and he let the humor soothe him, no matter that it killed his ribs.

"If you can laugh in the middle of this, I give you kudos." Cassie's voice was higher pitched than normal, and along with her constant fidgeting, revealed her uneasiness. She remained cocooned in her bag save for her face, which she'd just poked out. "I'm freezing, Daniel."

He stoked the fire. "I know. This fire can't keep up with the storm." He met her gaze and knew she saw the same concern, the constant discomfort of trying to stay warm. They were still eating, had enough water and pushed one another to consume as much as their stomachs could handle. It was a key to survival to remain hydrated and fueled. But so was staying dry, and as shivers hit him, he knew the deepest fear since right before their helicopter plunged into the icy lake. Hypothermia.

"What are we going to do?" Cassie was seated, and she used her legs and arms inside her bag to shake the snow off. The large, wet stains left behind on the fabric attested to their danger.

"We're going to stay as warm as we can. We'll take turns sleeping, like before, and keep the snow off the tarp. We'll get through the night, Cassie, one hour at a time."

She nodded. "I believe you, Daniel."

Ten minutes later they'd both taken care of nature's call. Cassie had thought her skin was going to fall off from the cold and found zero comfort in her wet layers.

She and Daniel sat across from one another, with the fire in between them. Daniel had added more wood to it but his previous observation was correct. It was hard for any fire to compete with the brutal blizzard raging around them.

"I never thought I'd see a snowstorm like this in August." Her throat hurt from shouting over the almost fifteen feet between them. But she needed to keep talking, needed to hear Daniel. Daniel's voice soothed her in a way she couldn't explain.

"I'd have preferred to come here as soon as the park opened, in June, because I figured I'd need all summer to dig the wreck out. But I couldn't get up here sooner. The flights have been spotty at best." Daniel's sentiment mirrored her own.

"I'm thrilled I even made it this year. I've been saving for a big trip for a long while, and it only came to me to do this for my grandmother last fall. When I realized she was going to be eighty-five, and how much she'd always missed having a place to remember her mother by, the full circle most of us get when we bury our loved ones, I knew I had to do it. I never expected to actually see where Eugenia's soul left the earth, though. Certainly not in a snowstorm!"

"And here we are. It's a generous gift you're giving Grandma Rose and your entire family, Cassie." The appreciation in his voice resonated in her heart and for the first time all night, heat raced to her cheeks. A slower rush than normal, but she welcomed any validation that her body was warming up.

"It may have been, but now I have to wonder at my own ignorance. It was pure ego to do this. I'd saved the money, sure, and I enjoy seeing new places, especially where I can get out in nature. This, though, is a bit much."

His laugh made his shoulders shake, visible through the snow and flickering flames. She joined in.

"You may have been egged on by your ego, but it's your love that makes this trip special."

"Maybe."

As their laughter and conversation ebbed, she was content to stare into the fire. A while later, it could have been minutes or hours, she had no idea, Cassie looked at her watch. The digital numbers cast an eerie glow in the darkness.

"We've got another hour until dawn."

"I'm not certain we'll see a big difference in the light, depending on the cloud cover." As he spoke a large *boom* split the air, followed by a shudder through the ground they sat on.

"It's the wind. It sounds like it knocked down another tree." She shouted the obvious over the wind's howls, but couldn't get herself to calm down. The pitch rose and more *thuds* and *bangs* happened. Each time she felt the tremors of the earth under her and feared they'd be squashed like bugs with the next gust. Cold seeped into her limbs and her toes, her feet, grew numb. "We have to move around."

"Yes." Daniel's reply was a harsh grunt and she knew his ribs had to be on fire.

"I can help you get up. Lean on me. I'm stronger than I look." She yelled at him, hoping her feigned enthusiasm would take his mind off the pain. Struggling to her feet, she knew it would be far worse for Daniel. The several steps around the fire to him felt like moon steps, and her footprints looked like it in the packed white snow.

"Thanks." He grasped her hand as she braced her back against a tree. It was unnerving to feel how much the tree swayed with the wind. As they'd hiked into this forest it had enveloped them. Each tree seemed connected to the other. The harsh winds had died and there had been a sense of safety she hadn't had since their crash.

Now the very thing she'd found as a source of strength—the trees—threatened their lives.

She mustered all her strength to support Daniel's weight as he stood. "You've got this. Take your time."

"I'm okay." His breath came out in forceful blows against her cheeks, another worrying sign. There was no use suggesting he rest; it was impossible for a human being to sleep while the world fell down around them. And the cold. She couldn't stop the shivers that had returned, the way her teeth were chattering.

Finally he was upright and they faced one another, the gale rushing around them. Would this be their last moments alive?

He rubbed her upper arms. "This will pass, Cassie. May I give you a hug?"

"Of course, but don't hurt yourself."

"Being with you is an antidote to all that ails me." He gently tugged her close and she stepped into the embrace, needing the reassurance of his strength, their friendship.

Maybe it was more than a friendship, but she had no energy to devote to that contemplation. They had to live through this night first.

Thud. More shudders through the ground, reaching up her legs.

"We can't stop this storm, Daniel." Desperation clawed at her bearing.

"There is one who can." He dropped his arms from around her, took her hands in his. They were surprisingly warm, which lifted her glum state. "Let's pray, Cassie."

They agreed on a prayer they'd each memorized

in childhood, after which they used words from their hearts. Cassie had never had occasion to experience tranquility amid such a frightening circumstance. This trip was all about firsts. After they finished their conversation with God, they stood in one another's arms, waiting for the next tree to fall. Cassie prayed a tree wouldn't crush them, that this wasn't her last night on earth.

It was the most difficult time she'd ever had to turn her will over.

Your will, not mine, Father.

Chapter Thirteen

Daniel could have stayed with Cassie, complaining ribs notwithstanding. The worries of their journey, the ongoing storm, melted away with their prayers. He'd not prayed as much with his former girlfriends as he had with Cassie these last days and he realized he'd missed out on something very special. Of course, Cassie had something to do with it, too. Her easy manner and openness to being in the moment with God were a comfort, no matter how rough their chances of hiking out of here alive got.

She fit perfectly under his chin, her long hair tied back in a ponytail and trailing down her back. His fingers toyed with the strands as he tried to hold her as gently as possible. Sure, his ribs were sore, but he knew she wasn't letting on how much her bones must hurt, too. When her teeth stopped chattering, he let out a long sigh of relief.

"Warming up?"

Her head rubbed against his jaw. "Yes, thank you.

I think sitting on the cold ground, even with our mats, wasn't helping."

"Being in one position is the worst. And we don't have dry clothes to change into, which doesn't help."

"My clothes aren't bothering me as much as they were. The warmth helps. I don't suppose our fire's going to make it, is it?"

"It doesn't matter. As soon as we're warmed up, we're walking out."

"In the storm?"

"I'm hoping it lets up, but yes, we have to keep going, Cassie. My GPS is still working, and I have the maps. If it's a total white-out, we'll pause as needed. But we can't let one day pass without moving."

Her silence weighed heavy on his heart, and the ache inside his chest had nothing to do with his ribs.

"Cassie?" He felt for her face, which was wet with tears. He longed to give her the comfort her presence had provided him through all of this. Using his calloused fingers to wipe her cheeks was the best he had.

"It's okay, I know we need to head out. I'd hoped for a chance to search the wreckage, is all. You know, in the off chance there's anything Eugenia left behind. I'll get over it."

Ouch. More soul wrenching. One thing he'd never liked was how much it hurt him when the person he cared about was in pain. A way to protect himself had been to keep people out, to not allow himself to open up to a woman as he was doing with Cassie.

When had she become so important to him? Why? *Help Cassie.*

"Do you have comfort that Eugenia's soul's at rest, with God?"

"Yes, I do. This really isn't about her, though, is it? Or me. It's about my grandmother, who grew up motherless, and my mother, who never knew her grandmother. It's hard to explain but the specter of grief that's overshadowed our family reaches to me, my sisters."

"I do understand, at least the grief part. My family has a history of alcoholism and there are relatives I've never known, some still alive but incommunicado with any of us due to some pretty rough issues." He heard his words and stopped. "I'm sorry. I really have no idea what you're going through, what your family feels. No one in mine served in World War II, as their generations didn't match up to the service dates. Plus it sounds like your grandmother had your mom later than mine. My grandmother was married at sixteen and had my mother when she was seventeen."

"Yes, your grandmother was younger than mine. But a mother, a grandmother, is the same, no matter the age. Love doesn't know what birthday it is. And your family's missing pieces are just as painful and gaping as mine. The feeling that there's more to the story, there are people you should know better than you do. That's exactly what it's like."

"If it's any consolation, there's little to no chance we'd find anything, even if we could get into the cabin, past all the overgrowth." He was loath to add that wildlife would have taken care of her grandmother's body and any passengers onboard. "Do you know if she was flying alone?"

"I'm not certain, but from the records I saw, there

were probably a few others with her. It was a long flight, from the UK to Newfoundland, then Massachusetts. She'd only been near the end of the first leg."

"There's still a chance a local might know something or remember their elder family members talking about it."

She sniffed, and her hands were on his chest. Lightly, as if afraid he'd shatter. Truth be told, his ribs never felt better than when he was near her. "Maybe. I would like to leave the plaque I brought here, nonetheless. What you said earlier makes the most sense. It's wonderful that I've been able to find her airframe, and it's the best place to leave it."

"I think that's a great idea." He was awed at the devotion in her voice, and her family's tight ties that would plan for her to be able to honor her great-grandmother in such a real way, thousands of miles from home, decades—almost a century—since she'd passed on.

"Hey, listen. Morning's here." Her hushed tone was overflowing with hope.

The woods had once again grown quiet. As quickly as the storm had turned into something life-threatening, it had stopped. The silence was surreal after the screaming gale. His ears were still ringing from the storm but he thought he heard birds chirping.

"Sounds like dawn. Let's take a look." They both looked up to the ever-lightening sky. To no precipitation.

"It's stopped!" Her glee reflected his relief. But instead of having a surge of adrenaline to help him get going, it was as if he was one hundred years old, ready to take a long winter's nap.

He mentally shook the exhaustion off. It was nothing

more than the stress of it all. Of course the thought of
staying in place with Cassie appealed, too. But his logic
had convinced him that pursuing any line of thought
that included them seeing one another after this remained a fool's errand. Cassie was a family girl, and
he didn't see her leaving central PA. He was devoted
to his family, too, four hours away from her. The miles
weren't more than a few hundred, but were they both
willing to make whatever sacrifices or compromises it
might take to see one another after this? After knowing one another for such a short time?

As close as they felt now, wouldn't it fade into their
memories, a lost adventure to tell future grandkids
about?

With a pang he knew he'd like nothing more than
for the story to be told to *their* grandchildren. His and
Cassie's.

But this wasn't the time to think about it, to bring
it up.

You're making excuses.

Maybe he was, but he couldn't dwell on it. Not now.
At least not until he had her safe and sound at Base
Camp. And after that, he might figure out what he was
feeling for her was nothing more than circumstance.

Fat chance.

Like Cassie, he didn't believe in coincidence. What
he knew was that he'd never live with himself, alone or
otherwise, if anything happened to her.

With daylight and the end of the storm came clarity
for Cassie. She'd accomplished what she'd come here

for, save getting to Base Camp. Daniel was right; moving on and hiking out was the only choice.

"Here it is. I got permission from the proper authorities, local and national, to leave this. Only, I never dared hope it would be at the actual crash site." Cassie pulled the plaque from the bubble wrap bag she'd wrapped it in the night before she'd flown out of Harrisburg Airport. She held it up so that Daniel could read it with her.

Eugenia Smith Haas
Beloved Wife, Daughter, Mother and Faithful
Servant
November 6, 1919–August 17, 1942

"That's beautiful, Cassie."

"I'm sorry I didn't think of tracking down the other families. I could have brought them all closure." Voicing her regret made it more bearable, with Daniel at her side.

"You said you tried to find out who the other passengers were, though. You can't take responsibility for everything." His forgiving countenance was another aspect of Daniel she wouldn't forget.

"You mean like you have this entire trip?" She couldn't help teasing; it was natural to banter with him.

He grinned. "I suppose I have."

"Hey, no complaints from me. Your sense of accountability saved our lives."

"It takes all three of us." He pointed up at the sky so she knew what he meant. God was the most important being here. The reminder buoyed her, gave her strength to do what she'd come here to do.

"Will you take a photo of me with the plaque? I'll shoot a bunch of pics before we walk out." They'd already packed up the minimal camp, eager to make time as long as the weather held.

"I'll use my camera and share them with you." He reached for his small kit of lightweight, professional equipment, tools for his historical search jobs. "I've gotten hundreds of shots of the aircraft, yesterday and now. They're all yours as soon as we're back."

"Thanks." She thought it'd be a quick snap but Daniel, ever the detail man, took his time, asked her to stand this way and that. She placed the plaque atop the fuselage, where it seemed natural. When the plane decayed further, the makeshift grave marker would decompose with it, which suited her and paid respect to Eugenia and her ultimate sacrifice.

"Stay there for a minute more, with your hands on the plaque."

As he captured the occasion her grandmother had only ever dreamed of, she began to silently weep. Hot tears streamed down her face but she didn't swipe at them, hoping to not ruin the photos.

"Cass."

Their gazes met, held. So much empathy, compassion in his. What did he see in hers? Grief, yes, but could he tell what he was becoming to mean to her?

"It's all right—I'm fine. These are more tears of joy than anything. Being tired and cranky isn't helping my state, for certain. We haven't even made our usual gourmet coffee." She referred to the instant powder they'd had once or twice, not wanting to waste water. Her weak attempt at levity was rewarded with his soft smile. He lowered the camera and took the several steps to her. His hands cupped her face, his thumbs gently removing her tears. The sweet gesture made her tears flow all the more.

"I'm so proud of you, Cassie." His voice was full of conviction as it rumbled from his chest. "I've never met a woman willing to go to any lengths for her family, and to think it's for a woman you never met..." He shook his head, his own eyes glittering with what she knew were tears. How many men were strong enough to show their vulnerability?

Daniel. He was the strongest man she'd ever met. The most caring, too.

"Thank you. But—"

"Can I kiss you?" Daniel's query reached into her heart, filled her with quiet joy.

"Yes." She met him halfway. When their lips met it was as if they'd done this before, as if it were the most natural thing to do while stranded in the wilderness, placing her great-grandmother's equivalent of a headstone at the B-17 wreckage. The connection was warm, delicious, healing.

Her time with Daniel had healed her. Of a broken heart, of the grief her family had carried through the generations.

The realization shook her and she stepped back, her eyes on his face, wondering if he knew. Daniel had done what no amount of girls' nights out could touch, no heart searching had done. He'd helped her forget all about Jim and how badly she'd thought her heart had been trampled. It seemed ludicrous that she'd ever believed that was what a broken heart felt like. Because she'd only had a sliver of what she knew it was going to feel like when her time with Daniel was over. When the man who'd put her back together had to go back to his life, and she to hers.

Daniel had made it clear from the get-go that he had no time for a relationship. He was all about teaching and in the summers, history hunting. Not to mention Pittsburgh, four hours from her life. And more than all of the logistical issues, Daniel's heart had been stomped on too many times. He wasn't interested.

"Thank you for letting me kiss you, Cassie." His brown eyes remained on her but she couldn't read them; he'd shuttered them and their bond was back to where they'd begun. All business.

"No thanks are necessary. It's natural to want validation that we're alive, when surrounded by evidence of, um…" She didn't want to let him know how worried she was. The thoughts that maybe they wouldn't make it, only kept at bay by her, and her and Daniel's, prayers.

"You mean while the reminder that we could die at any wrong turn or move is in our faces? You're right. It's validation, nothing more." His expression revealed nothing, but was that a thread of hurt in his voice?

A snap sounded nearby, followed by scuffling, cutting off their conversation. They both stilled, and she was at once relieved and alarmed when Daniel reached for the rifle, which he'd rested against his leg.

"Hello?" A strange voice came out of the woods, and for a second Cassie wondered if she was dehydrated, hallucinating. Until the figures of two men emerged.

Rescuers!

"I'm Bill and this is my son Trevor." An older man, whom Cassie placed in his late thirties or early forties from the laugh lines at his eyes and silvering hair, nodded to the teenager, who looked like his father but had raven-black hair. "Are you Daniel and Cassie?"

"We are." Daniel and Cassie spoke in unison, and Cassie let the tightness across her chest ease. It wasn't a brown or polar bear, but two human beings. They looked far fresher and stronger than she felt.

Bill's mouth broke into a huge grin. "We've been looking for you for the last two days."

"Only the last two?" They'd crashed four days ago. Daniel had been right; no one was sent to save them right away.

"The weather's been a bear, for certain. I'm one of the Inuit guides with Base Camp, and Trevor's in training. We were taking a break at the small village my folks are from, not far from Way Point, when we got the call that a helicopter had gone down." Bill and Trevor both swung their gazes behind Cassie and Daniel. "Is Sean with you?"

"No. Did you know him?" Daniel's voice was steady, compassionate.

Bill nodded. "It's a close-knit community in these parts. Sean has been flying out of Nain for almost three decades. Ever since I was Trevor's age, for certain."

"I'm so sorry for your loss. He died a hero, trying to save us. If he hadn't maneuvered the helicopter into the lake, I'm not certain we'd be standing here talking to you." As Daniel broke the tragedy, Cassie had nothing to offer these strangers except her sincere sympathy and she felt at a loss. Back at home she'd make them a cup of tea, at least.

"It sounds just like Sean." Bill looked at the ground, leaning against his hiking poles. His reaction underscored that Sean's display of no-nonsense manners and dedication to his job hadn't been a one-time act for her and Daniel. This community had lost a valued friend four days ago.

"You okay?" Daniel spoke to Trevor, standing stock-still next to his father.

"Yeah, I'm good. Sean was a great man, like Dad said."

Cassie became aware that she was the only woman in the group, and that maybe she'd better make sure she had some kind of weapon available. Bill and Trevor seemed like the real deal, a father and son team who'd been sent to find them. But how could she be certain? Daniel had referred to some kind of historical treasure above and beyond the B-17 wreck. What if Bill and Trevor were another treasure-hunting team, out to find the priceless items themselves?

She believed God gave her common sense and a good bit of intuition, though. Cassie also believed that the gift of her mind was to be used, too. She had faith that He was keeping her and Daniel safe, but it didn't stop her from feeling for the can of bear spray in her vest pocket. She hated having to be afraid of people when all they'd hoped for since the crash was being found, rescued.

Daniel. He'd help her keep her head screwed on straight. She turned to see what he was thinking but no one was beside her. Bill and Trevor let out short barks of warning.

"Catch him!"

"Whoa!"

Daniel had crumpled to the ground, unconscious.

Chapter Fourteen

"He's dehydrated, most likely." Cassie's worried voice reached him from the black pit he'd sunk into. One minute he'd been ready to get dinner going, the next he was on his back, three pairs of eyes peering at him with only the campfire to light their concerned faces.

Cassie.

"I'm good." He moved to sit up but the pain in his back, just under his rib cage, was too sharp, his breath too short. He might be paying for this adventure for weeks to come. But it'd been worth it. They'd found the wreck.

Memories flooded in and panic gripped him. Were Bill and Trevor looking for the treasure, too? He had to warn Cassie.

"Stay still. Here." Cassie held her water bottle to his lips and patiently waited for him to sip. "Keep going." She wouldn't stop until he'd finished the rest of it, which made his anxiety ratchet up several notches. The worry in her eyes made him want to put his arms around her again, comfort her. Yet if she worried about Bill and

Trevor's true motives, she didn't show it. She appeared concerned about his health, but nothing more. Her face turned from his as she addressed the other two.

"How close are we to the town you were talking about? Is there a doctor there?"

"It's a two-day hike. And it's not a town, more like a small outpost."

Her face fell as did his stomach. Two more days to any kind of civilization made his ribs ache all the more. But it wasn't time to give up, or in. "I'll be fine in a minute. We've been going for four days straight, is all."

"You need a night of rest and warmth. There's no hiking today, forget it. It's cleared up in this area but the storm is still all around us. It could start snowing again in a flash." Bill's voice sounded experienced, at least. And if they'd had to hike two days to reach them, the man knew his way around the Torngat Mountains.

"You'll be able to sleep tonight, since the three of us can take over the watch." As she spoke to him, Cassie's open trust bothered him, but he knew she wasn't a fool, and wouldn't be tricked by Bill and Trevor if their motives turned out to be nefarious.

"I can manage a watch." No way was he going to sleep while two strange men were in camp with them.

"Cassie's right, Daniel." Bill gave off an aura of calm knowledge, but Daniel didn't know if he could trust his judgment when he was in pain and dehydrated. "We can handle the watch. There's no getting out of here tonight with this storm, and we'll hopefully break camp tomorrow. Storm's supposed to last three days and we're not even through two yet."

"A three-day snowstorm in August. Who back home

will ever believe me?" Cassie's incredulity brought a smile to his face. She'd done her research but the weather was never predictable here.

"It'll turn to rain by tomorrow afternoon, then clear out, if we're so blessed." Bill turned to Trevor. "Let's get our camp set up. We'll make our own fire, keep the heat going all night." Trevor disappeared, but not before he took his father's pack and carried it with his. The simple sight of easy strength made Daniel's ribs ache. Maybe he did need more rest tonight. And ibuprofen.

"Here. Take these and then eat this." Cassie was pressing two tablets into his palm, under his glove, and set a protein bar next to a full water bottle.

"You're going to need more water."

"I'm good, I've still got a bottle and a half. We should have been drinking more all day. And guess what? Bill and Trevor brought two sets of dry long underwear, one for each of us. Plus dry socks!"

Daniel grunted and swallowed the pills. He didn't need the reminder of his failure as a guide for Cassie today. It weighed heavy on his soul that he could have cost them both their lives through the sheer negligence of getting dehydrated and hypothermia.

He had no idea if he was really dehydrated. A thought kept tugging at his mind that maybe his ribs were more than bruised. And if he'd fractured one, or two, the possibility that he'd incurred internal bleeding had to be faced. He slowly maneuvered into a seated position, praying the dizziness wouldn't come back. If he was losing blood, there was no way he'd be able to walk out of here on his own.

Who'd be here to protect Cassie then? Fear more

powerful than facing down a bear ricocheted through him and landed in a pit in his gut.

No. He wasn't going to let anything happen to her. *Please, God.*

Cassie decided the best way to survive the night alone with two strangers was prayer. She prayed when she had to find privacy out of the camp to tend to herself; she prayed while she made sure Daniel was close enough to the fire to stay warm all night; she prayed during her turn to keep watch over the camp, after assuring Bill that she knew how to use the rifle and wouldn't hesitate if a bear threatened them.

And she prayed that Bill and Trevor were who they claimed: two locals who'd heard of the crash and set out to see whom they could rescue. As night turned to dawn, she was too tired to care about anything but getting Daniel to a safe place and checked out by a doctor.

"Is there a medical professional in the outpost we're going to?" She spoke to Bill over a cup of hot coffee, thanks to her instant powder and the inches of snow available for the beverages. Trevor and Daniel were still asleep.

"There's a healer, but she's farther out, in an actual village. Her granddaughter is the local pilot and has studied healing under her elder. A few folks are trained EMTs, but we do have a local medic of sorts, Gus. No doctor until we're at the base camp."

"How far of a hike is it to Base Camp from there?" She was afraid to ask, unsure if Daniel was going to make it.

"Oh, you don't have to hike from there. We have

ATVs and with extra fuel along for the ride, we can be there in less than one day, weather permitting."

She let out a sigh of relief. Finally, a sliver of hope. *Thank You, God.*

Cassie counted seven buildings total when they came to the mini-village of Way Point. Or outpost, as Bill had called it. Four were prefabricated units not unlike double-wide trailers in the US, only bigger, with wooden steps for each. The other three buildings looked like cabins, several of which they'd passed on the way in over the last few hours. Bill had explained that Way Point was originally a Labradorimiut settlement that managed to survive being moved twice and was having a rebirth of sorts due to ecotourism. It helped support Base Camp during the very short, but tourist-laden, summer weeks.

"I've been to places like this here before, and in other parts north of the Arctic Circle." Daniel hadn't faltered once over the last two days and she marveled at his grit.

"You'd think we were in the Arctic with how cold it gets." Since this morning the temperatures had risen into what she considered more seasonal, in the low sixties. Or twenties, going by the Celsius scale used in Canada. As predicted, all of the snow had melted off by end of day yesterday.

"It could get cold again, but this is amazing, isn't it?" Daniel kept pace but when he spoke, he huffed and puffed like an old man. She placed her hand on his forearm.

"You can stop being the hero now. We're safe, Bill

and Trevor are wonderful, and we're going to be well taken care of."

They stopped when they caught up to their rescuers.

"First stop for you both. But before you split up, you may want to see if you have cell phone reception. Most of us get it here. Don't ask me why here and not only a few miles out into the woods. But I'd guess your families were informed of the helicopter disappearing and told of a probable crash. They'll be awfully glad to hear from you."

Cassie wasted no time in pulling out her phone and turning the power on. At first she wasn't showing any bars, but after a few minutes, one, then two, bars appeared. Relief and vulnerability overwhelmed her. Her finger shook as she poked in her mother's cell contact.

"Cassie?" Her mom's voice was so high-pitched, so strained, it shook right through Cassie's reserve as she acknowledged the sheer torture her parents must have been through.

"Mom." She gasped on a sob. "I'm okay."

"Oh, thank the dear Lord. Tom! It's Cassie!" She made out her father's bass tone, but not much else, due to either the fragile connection or the frenetic relief on both sides.

"Cassie." Her father's single word had her sinking to her knees, grateful to God for this second chance at life, and that her parents no longer had to worry about her.

"Hi, Daddy. I'm at an outpost, and we're going to the base camp I was supposed to land at…" She mentally counted. Had it been almost a week? "Last week."

"Well, isn't this a blessing from above. We're both so happy to hear from you. I told your mother that since we hadn't heard anything since the first call, and the weather had been so bad up there, that I was certain you'd found your way out of wherever you were." Her daddy's words were comforting but the way his voice shook betrayed his deep concern.

"I'm so sorry that I've worried you. I tried to call many times but we didn't have a signal until now."

"Your mother's been in constant prayer since we had the call, Cassie. I'd say this is one prayer that was answered, right, Dottie?"

She heard her mother laugh, and the sound of pure joy buoyed her flagging spirits. It had indeed been the longest week of her life.

And the most revealing. Before she'd met Daniel, Cassie's story at least to herself and her family was that she wasn't looking for a boyfriend, or someone to date. Not after Jim's awful abuse of her trust. Yet now, it was as if she'd matured tenfold in the past week.

Cassie ended the call with her parents only after making them promise to tell Grandma Rose she'd found Eugenia's plane, and assured them she'd call again once at Base Camp.

She stared at her phone screen once the call ended, unable to let go of her revelation. It wasn't simply the struggles and challenges she'd faced with Daniel, or their circumstances, so often dire. It was that they'd done it together. Each and every bit of it. Cassie had never felt as though Daniel was treating her like anything but his full partner in survival. She hoped he'd experienced the same with her. She sought him out, wanting to ask him, needing to tell him her heart, but he was striding toward Bill, who stood several yards ahead of them, waiting for them to catch up. Disappointment struck as she saw this wasn't the time to share her deepest thoughts with Daniel. She slowed her steps and stood next to Bill, who nodded at them both.

"Welcome to our home on the range. The clinic's there. Daniel, you need to see our local doc first, I'd say."

"At your local clinic?"

Bill grinned. "It's a clinic of sorts. A retired army medic runs it. With help from the healer. They can fix most of whatever's the problem, trust me. No fancy machines, but they'll know if you need to get medevac'd or not."

"Or not?" Daniel's stubbornness belied the white patches on his face. Cassie recognized them as she got them after a particularly rough hike back home, or after one of the 10K races she liked to participate in to stay in shape.

"As I've told you, we'll get you to Base Camp tomorrow on our ATVs." He pointed to a group of several of the motorized four-wheelers, lined up near another pre fabricated building.

"They look like fun." Cassie meant it. She'd be happy to ride an elephant if it meant she didn't have to hike for a day.

"Trevor, take Cassie to our place. Mom will feed her and let her use up the hot water. I've got Daniel. We'll eat with Gus."

Cassie looked at Daniel. It was the first time she was going to be away from him, his protection, since before the crash. She tried to put on a brave face, but fear sidled over her serenity. "Good luck with the docs."

"I'm going to catch up with you at Bill's place, Cass." Daniel looked at Bill. "Right?"

"Right. We have plenty of space. You'll be on the sofa, and Cassie, you can take Trevor's room. Trevor will stay in the living room with Daniel. You both need a good rest after the last two days, not counting the several you were on your own before we found you. And best of all, we have some decent chow, right, Trevor?"

Trevor, typical of an adolescent, had been quiet through much of their hike to this outpost. When Bill mentioned food, though, his eyes lit up and he let out a whoop. "Stew tonight! And nachos!"

Cassie couldn't stop her mouth from watering if she wanted to. Never had the two meals sounded like filet mignon and sushi used to.

Daniel reached for her hand and squeezed it gently, letting her know she'd be okay. "I'll be right here, in that building." He pointed at the clinic. "Come get me if you need me. I shouldn't be long."

"Thanks." She returned his smile and wondered if he had the same butterflies skimming around his insides. It'd be easy to blame her nervousness on finally being rescued, going to another unknown at Bill's place.

As she fell into step alongside Trevor she let her defenses down and admitted to herself what she might never tell anyone else.

The emotion that flowed through her every time she looked at Daniel had nothing to do with the fact they'd been through a unique crisis together. It added to the urgency of her emotions, for certain, but all she needed to do was remember how she'd felt each time they'd prayed together. Solid. Safe. Loved.

Yes, she'd fallen for her mountain protector.

Chapter Fifteen

"I think you've cracked at least two ribs, maybe more."
The grizzled face didn't do the bright eyes justice as
a man Daniel estimated must have been a medic in
World War I, even though he knew that was impossible, pressed his hands on his abdomen, felt along his rib
cage, checked all of his limbs. "No X-ray machine but
your lungs will tell me what I need to know." He pulled
out a stethoscope and told Daniel to breathe normally.

"Okay, now take the deepest breath you can without it hurting."

"That would be not breathing."

"Funny guy." Gus pressed the metal disc against
Daniel's lower back and Daniel jumped.

"Whoa! What was that?"

Gus straightened up and looked him in the eye.
The man had cataracts thicker than Daniel's parents'
thirteen-year-old dog. But it didn't keep his keen gaze
from striking terror into Daniel.

"Hmph. Here, sit up straighter." Gus waited for him
to comply, then used his hands to lightly tap Daniel on

his back, just below his ribs. Pain shot through him, making the rib cage injury seem like a paper cut.

"Ow. What on earth is wrong?" Was he dying?

"Kidney infection is my guess. Makes sense with you passing out from dehydration. We have some antibiotics here. I'll give you enough for two days, and Base Camp can help out with the rest. It's not uncommon when folks get stuck out here. Water's all around but it's easy to fall off the recommended eight-a-day."

"So you don't think I punctured a lung?"

Gus shook his head. "Naw, doesn't sound like it. You've got some deep gashes on your legs, from the helo crash I suppose?"

Daniel nodded. "They stopped bleeding quickly enough."

"And you applied the glue and butterfly bandages, so they're healing well. You'll have scars, of course. I'll need to check out your wife, too."

"Uh, she's not my wife." But did he wish she was?

"Girlfriend?"

"Ah, no. We met on the helicopter, basically."

Gus crossed his arms in front of him, rocked back on his heels. "Is that so? It looked like you got along well enough." At Daniel's expression, he laughed. "Son, nothing's a secret out here. We all—all sixteen of us in this outpost—watched from our windows as you walked in. You're our biggest news next to the polar bear."

"Polar bear?"

"You didn't know? I thought Bill would have mentioned it. We've had several sightings of a mother and cub. Now before you start thinking of a cuddly little guy, know that an Inuk cub is forty-five kilos at eight months, which is this guy's age. The mother's been in and out of here for years, bringing her cubs when she has them."

"Has she ever attacked?"

"Humans? Not so as I know of. But with a cub, well, they're unpredictable."

"I carried electric fencing with me and used it each night. This is my third time up here."

"Yeah, you're the aircraft wreckage hunter, right? Is the B-17 Bill found you next to the one you were seeking?"

"Yeah, but in truth I need to go back."

"Let me guess, you think there's some kind of treasure there you need to find?" Gus's eyes twinkled with knowing, and Daniel wasn't sure if he liked it.

"Uh, as a matter of fact, I was headed to Base Camp to meet up with a guide, to find the same exact airframe. As it turns out, we ended up able to see it on our way here."

Gus washed his hands at the sink and addressed Daniel over his shoulder. "Don't you think people have come before you, looking for the same?"

"There's no record of this particular aircraft ever being found."

"'No record,' as in nothing on the internet?"

"As in I searched all the historical World War II records that are in existence regarding the Flying Fortress." He referred to the B-17's model name. "We know the ones who never made it home, and this wreck has all the signs of being the one I came to find. I'd like to spend more time with it."

"You need to get to Base Camp to make sure your

ribs aren't about to puncture a lung. Otherwise you'll be passing out from blood loss instead of dehydration." Gus turned and leaned back against the counter, but instead of crossing his arms this time he crossed his legs at his ankles and faced Daniel with a smile. "What do you need? To match the serial number of the plane that's on record?"

"We've already matched the serial number, and it corresponds to the correct aircraft call sign."

"So you are looking for something else."

Daniel remained silent, unwilling to share the exact terms of his contract. Some items he searched for he couldn't mention because of the NDA, but also, he didn't know Gus, or Bill, from Adam.

"Don't answer, I get it. I'm a history buff myself, and hike out to spots when they find stuff, which since you've done the research you know isn't uncommon. My only suggestion is that you go to Base Camp first, get checked out. And before you leave here, meet with Amy McGill."

"Who's she?"

"My partner in crime. She's the local Inuit healer and pilot. Her grandparents originally found your B-17 right after it crashed. Amy flies mail in and out from here to Base Camp to Nain and back, several times a week. Trust me, she's the gal you want to talk to. I'll take you over there once you shower and we feed you. Bill's swinging back to join us for lunch."

"Thank you." Hope sparked that he'd get more information on the treasure but it was overshadowed by his disappointment at being away from Cassie that much longer as he put his jacket back on. He felt emotionally naked without her at his side, no matter that she was only a few buildings away. Had to be another side effect of fighting for their lives together the better part of a week. Gus opened a cabinet with a key and took out a bottle. He measured out several large pills and placed them in a small white envelope.

"Take one now, then one at dinner, one at bedtime. Tomorrow take one every six hours. You'll be back at Base Camp by then, where they'll give you the rest of the week's worth. And drink water like your life depends on it. Your kidneys are precious, son."

"Thanks, sir." He reached out a hand and Gus took it.

"I'm Gus. Just Gus."

Bill's wife, Ramona, turned out to be a fiber artist. She'd joined her husband and son at the outpost so that she could finish a book of knitting patterns over the summer. Cassie didn't understand how the woman had willingly left civilization and agreed to live in such a remote place for three months, But then again, not a lot of people would use their life savings to come to the same spot in search of something the odds were against them finding. And yet, she'd most likely seen Great-grandma Eugenia's B-17. The memory of it made tears rush to her eyes.

"Oh, I'm so sorry." She dabbed at her eyes with a paper napkin. "It's been full-on waterworks lately and I have no clue why."

"It's okay, Cassie. You're bound to be exhausted and overwhelmed after your ordeal. Is there anything else I can do for you?" Ramona had made her three cups of tea since her arrival and fed her caribou stew with a hearty pumpernickel bread. From the shape of the loaf and pan atop the counter, Cassie figured Ramona had baked it herself.

"No, you've been so wonderful and welcoming. I feel like I'm home."

Ramona smiled. "A tent would feel great after what you've been through. Bill said you and your partner had already been hiking for several days when they found you, and then you made the two-day trek here. You were on Sean's flight?"

"Yes. I'm so sorry for your loss." Regret filled her and she put the slice she'd buttered down. "Did you know Sean well, too?"

"Not as well as Bill and Trevor. I usually stay at our winter home, near Quebec City, in the summers and let them do their wilderness time. But my mother passed last spring and our daughter is in Europe for her university's summer study program. I didn't want to be alone, yet I needed the time and space to meet my deadline." Ramona looked around the bare-bones trailer. "It's rough, sure, but I have my laptop, power, and Wi-Fi. I use my cell phone as a hot spot. You're welcome to use it as you need to."

"Thank you. I've noticed since I got here that my phone has two bars."

"Have you contacted your family?"

"Yes, as soon as I had the reception." Tears welled again. The pure love in her parents' voices wrapped around her all over again.

"I'll bet they were happy to hear from you!" Ramona stood up and cleared the table of the extra plates, placed them on the sideboard. "I'll wash these in a bit.

I'm going to see where my men have disappeared to and bring back more meat for dinner. They hunt caribou this time of year, and the storage freezers are in a small airplane hangar."

"Yes, I saw it on the walk in. Who's the pilot?" And she wondered why they couldn't be flown to Base Camp tomorrow instead of taking ATVs. Although getting in an airplane wasn't tops on her list.

"Amy. She brings the mail in and out. But her plane is only a single seater, not enough room for any passengers, just a big duffel of mail and supplies."

"It would be nice to have a shorter trip than all day tomorrow."

"Agreed, but you'll see beautiful scenery along the way. By the way, Bill texted me and you're to meet Daniel at Amy's after you shower. Daniel's having a meal with Gus. Do you want to see him, too? It's probably a good idea."

She shook her head. "No, I'm fine, honest. Since we'll be at Base Camp tomorrow, I can wait until then. The only things still bothering me are sore muscles, and I don't think there's anything to do for them but time."

"A hot shower will help. I'm sorry we don't have a bathtub here, but the stall is a good size and we have an extra tank of water. The heater's a flash, so no worries about using up hot water. Please take your time in the shower and help yourself to the soap and shampoo. You might prefer mine, in the nicer containers, than Bill and Trevor's all-in-one sandalwood." She grinned.

"Will do. Thank you."

Ramona left and Cassie went to the shower. As achy and sore as she still was from the last days, she undressed as quickly as possible and got herself under the gloriously strong spray. Never had hot water felt so good.

Her mind wandered as she showered, over how each day had unfolded. The way Daniel had opened up to her, revealed so much of himself. She'd certainly been the most comfortable with him than she'd been with anyone besides her family, ever. Which led her thoughts back to what she wanted to tell him. But what would she say? That she cared? Of course she did. Was that enough to ask him to consider staying in touch—or maybe something more?

Chapter Sixteen

Amy McGill stood at the door of her trailer, a skeptical brow arched over dark brown eyes, shiny black hair tied back in a practical knot. She didn't appear to be much older than him and Cassie, who'd walked up to join him and Bill as they stood in front of Amy's place.

The sight of a fresh-scrubbed Cassie took his breath away. Her hair hung in long, wavy damp lengths and brought out the sapphire depths of her eyes. But it wasn't just that she was clean, or in clothes he hadn't seen before—probably from Bill's wife—no, not at all. It was the light in her eyes, the eagerness in her steps as she approached. Her gaze never left his, as if she'd been pained by their half-day separation, too.

"Hey." He greeted her quietly, not wanting to share this moment with Bill or Amy.

"Hi. How are you? Are your ribs fractured?" Cassie's smile was somber, as if she'd found out a secret she wasn't giving up yet.

"Gus thinks it's probable that there is a fracture or

two. He gave me meds for other stuff and I'll get an X-ray as soon as I can to be certain."

"Sounds good." She was friendly but he detected a detachment to her tone. Had he done something to upset her? With a start he realized that he was overthinking everything when it came to Cassie.

Because you can't stop thinking about her.

Man, he had to stop it. She didn't need a protector any longer; they were in the clear, on their way to civilization. This wasn't like him. Daniel prided himself on sticking to a plan, executing it to the best of his ability, delivering whatever his current employer asked for.

He couldn't stop wondering if she was okay, if there was anything he should be doing for her.

Probably your own version of shock from all that's happened.

"Daniel, Cassie, meet Amy. Amy, these are our intrepid explorers." Bill seemed oblivious to the undercurrents flowing between Daniel and Cassie.

"Welcome to our piece of the world." Amy's smile was welcoming. "Come on in."

"I'm going to see Ramona, take a shower. I'll see you two back at our place for dinner." Bill nodded at him and Cassie before turning to Amy. "Thanks, Amy."

"No problem, Bill." She held the metal door open and motioned for Cassie and Daniel to come in. "Make yourselves at home."

Amy's place was far more decorated and cozy than Gus's makeshift clinic and living spaces. Cassie sank into an easy chair and Daniel took one end of a sofa, leaning forward. He pulled the maps back out along with a waterproof notebook he'd written in from time to time, but especially once they found the B-17. He looked at Amy. "May I?" He motioned to the coffee table.

"Absolutely. I'm interested in what you found. The B-17?"

"Yes." He pulled out his camera and clicked through to the best shots he'd taken. "Here." He handed it to her.

"My camera's a similar model for shooting wild-life." She nodded past his shoulder and he looked behind him, to the wall above the sofa. An enlarged photo of a polar bear as it stood against the sunset, its nose in the air, clearly exploring, graced the wall. It was a stunning shot.

"That's amazing. When did you take that?" He couldn't keep the awe out of his voice.

"Last summer. I send away my digital files and get the prints mailed back. I have an online artist's site, too."

"I think I've been to your website." Cassie stood up and walked around the room, which Daniel now noticed was laden with photos of every conceivable kind of animal known in this area. "You have a photo of golden eagles next to a family of brown bears, right?"

Amy beamed. "Yes, that's mine. How did you find me?"

Cassie returned the smile and Daniel wished he could stare at it all night. There was nothing more comforting than Cassie's happiness. "I was researching this trip, trying to find out everything I could. I've been planning it for over a year."

"Neat. And you, Daniel? Did you just want to find the B-17?"

"We both did, actually. Cassie was looking for her

family's sake, and I spend my summers searching for historical landmarks including abandoned warplanes."

Both he and Cassie took turns explaining their motivations for traveling to Newfoundland-Labrador. Amy's expression remained kind and open the entire time, which Daniel took as a good sign. He wasn't certain if she'd be willing to share what she knew of the B-17 with a complete stranger.

"Well, first off, I want to say that I'm sorry no one could come look for you in the air. I don't do rescue ops per se but I do fly along the fjord as needed to spot stranded hikers. The weather was too bad when the distress call hit Base Camp, and then our equipment. By the time the visibility was good enough to search again, you were a day away with Bill and Trevor. I'm so glad they found you."

"We are, too." Cassie spoke up, seated again in the chair opposite Amy while Daniel looked at the maps and digested where they'd been, how far they'd hiked from the lake. "It was touch and go most of the days, frankly."

"But you both, or at least one of you, must know what you're doing. It's not unusual to lose hikers to the elements. Sometimes to bears." Amy didn't grimace or flinch when she said *bears*. He'd met several Inuit each summer he came here and had gotten to know the guide who'd taken him around two summers ago while he searched for a newer-model aircraft from the 1950s. He'd found no one had greater respect for the wildlife here than the Indigenous population, yet they also had a sense of ease he knew he'd never have when thinking about a bear confrontation scenario.

"Daniel is a survival expert. I was blessed to have

him to get us out of there alive." Cassie's voice grew softer as she spoke and her cheeks colored. He didn't have to see her eyes to know they shone with tears of gratitude. Cassie always blushed when she was about to cry.

He'd watched her tears fall several times these past days, as she had his. They'd truly been to the ends of the earth and back. Without her to stay focused on, and most importantly, God, he knew they'd have never made it. It would have been too easy to give up, especially when the weather had almost taken their lives the night before Bill and Trevor found them.

"Cassie's being modest. Without her common sense and grit, I would have lost my cool out there several times." As he spoke, Cassie looked at him and it was as if they were the only two in the room. She broke eye contact and turned to Amy.

"What do you know about the B-17, Amy? I'd love anything you have ever heard, to take back to my family."

"I have to admit, plenty of 'explorers'—" Amy made air quotes "—come up here each summer, thinking they'll be the ones to find a wreck or grave or see the one polar bear that no one else ever has. I grew up here, in a village not too far away, until I went to school. It's always wonderful to share in someone else's enthusiasm, but you two are different. I don't know a whole lot, but I do know that particular aircraft because my great-grandparents always told the story of how their parents saw the B-17 screech across the sky during a terrible storm. They heard it first, then caught a glimpse of it right before it hit the treetops. They were fishing on the fjord, you see."

Daniel stared at Amy. Did she realize she was telling Cassie about the last moments of her great-grandmother's life?

"Did, did they try to find the crew?" Cassie's mouth had gone dry as Amy spoke. It was a dream come true to find out more about Eugenia's final flight, but a nightmare, too.

Amy nodded. "Yes. They had to wait, as there was a fireball and when they found the plane it was too late to save anyone. There were three people on board, whom they buried on the spot as was customary at the time."

"So my great-grandmother was there?" She'd left the marker on the right spot. "But wait—I don't understand. Canada and the US are allies. Our War Department at the time, now the Defense Department, would have wanted to reclaim my great-grandmother's remains."

"They would have, for sure, but during the war communication wasn't what it is today. And in case you haven't already figured it out, we are truly in the middle of nowhere as far as most of the world is concerned." Amy's smile was gentle, compassionate. "I'm so sorry, Cassie."

Cassie blinked away tears. "There's nothing to be sorry about. It's a blessing that your ancestors found them, and that my ancestor had a proper burial. The best she could so far from home."

Thank You, God.

Amy looked from her to Daniel, then back again.

Her lips pursed and lines between her brows deepened as if she was trying to figure something out.

"Was there ever any talk about finding things aboard the aircraft? Or had it all been burned in the fire?" Daniel's query made her tense. Had whatever he was sent here to find been lost in a fire eighty years ago?

Amy let out a long sigh. "Yes. Give me a minute." She disappeared down a small hallway and they heard lots of shuffling, a few bangs against the thin walls. Cassie wondered how Amy stayed warm when the temperatures dropped, but then remembered this was only a summer station. Did Amy live in the village she'd mentioned the rest of the year?

She looked at Daniel. He was hunched over his notebook, writing furiously. His profile had become so dear to her, so familiar. Affection, respect and yearning rushed her heart as she watched him, so engrossed in his task. Only minutes earlier she'd been ready to share her newfound feelings with him. But no longer.

The courage to utter the words that best expressed what he was growing to mean to her had evaporated as Amy spoke. The reality of their situation fell upon her as heavy as the August snow they'd hiked through. Daniel had come here to find treasure. Rescuing her, both of them, had been a distraction. He'd put all his efforts into keeping them alive. But it was clear he was on to the entire reason he'd come to Torngat Mountains National Park in the first place.

Amy walked back in. "I'm sorry, you guys. I thought I might have something here that you'd be interested in. I'm going to have to call my grandmother and get back to you."

"I'll make sure you have my contact information." Daniel spoke up first.

"Oh, I won't need that. I take mail to the village I grew up in, where she still lives, tomorrow morning. I'll be waiting for you when you get to Base Camp. Again, sorry that my plane's too tiny to take either of you. But you'll enjoy the ATV trip."

Cassie wasn't certain she'd enjoy being bounced around for almost eight hours, and Daniel's ribs worried her. But he'd said Gus had told him he was good to go, so she wasn't going to say any more. Daniel was an adult, and she wasn't his mother. And it was clear God's plan had been at work.

Yes, this last week had changed her. For the first time, maybe ever, she was willing to share her heart with God alone. She needed time to see if her feelings for Daniel were only because of the intensity of their time together. And that meant going back home with no expectations of ever seeing him again.

Chapter Seventeen

Cassie walked around the living room as Amy made tea in the tiny kitchen. She paused the longest at the photos of a moose and cub, and an eagle in the moment after grabbing its prey, a fish nearly its size, in mustard-yellow talons. She was turned away from him and Daniel didn't like not seeing her expression, or the clear blue of her eyes. It was as if they'd developed a soul connection, something invisible yet as tangible as the way his side hurt with each breath.

He'd finished writing all the notes he possibly could from Amy's telling of the B-17's history. But he hadn't for one second forgotten the woman sitting across from him. Cassie had listened attentively to Amy and appeared more relaxed than he'd ever seen her. When they'd first met, she'd been nervous about the upcoming flight from Nain to the park's Base Camp. Except for the brief moments before it became clear the helicopter flight was doomed, he'd not seen what her usual countenance must be.

He couldn't handle one more second of not feeling

her gaze on him. How had it become everything to him? When he knew that she deserved a man who'd never want to leave her, not for all the historical treasures in the world?

Because he wasn't going to quit this part of his job; it was what he waited for each spring semester. He loved teaching and being there for his students. High school was hard when he went and hadn't gotten easier at all as technology and culture had a way of descending on adolescent brains in the most difficult ways. Daniel had thought he liked teaching because he'd been a good student, and education seemed a natural fit for him as he continued to college. But Cassie had him thinking about things from a different perspective. A more spiritual one. He'd thought he was intellectually above being called to a vocation, but wasn't that exactly what teaching was for him? And if so, where did that leave his treasure hunting summer job?

One thing was certain. He needed time alone back home to figure some things out. First thing would be going back to church. He thought his spiritual life was solid but Cassie had shown him how powerful prayer could be when he opened his heart all the way to fully rely on God. Not just talk to Him when it was convenient for Daniel.

"What are you thinking, Cassie?"

She turned from the photo of the eagles to answer him and he could think of nothing further than what a gift it had been to meet Cassie. How had he lived this long and not known she existed? Besides the obvious, that they lived in different cities and only ever would have met under these circumstances. The consideration in her gaze made him wonder if it wasn't just him and she was thinking some of the same deep thoughts he'd been.

A strong tug in the center of his chest that had nothing to do with his ribs made him sit up straighter, try to absorb each second with her. He knew they were among his last, as he'd not changed his mind about their connection, about trying to see if they could develop their bond further.

"I wouldn't call what my brain's doing anything close to thought." She giggled. "I think the exhaustion is catching up with me. But more than anything, I'm so grateful we ended up here. I never would have met Amy, unless by chance, at Base Camp."

"You said you don't believe in coincidence."

"I have no doubt this is a direct blessing from God. I'll be able to tell my grandmother everything she's longed to know about how her mother spent her last moments. And how she was treated with such respect after she died."

Cassie radiated a warmth born of faith that he could only ever hope to emulate. "I think you were put in my path to get me to remember what's really important. When I get home, I'm definitely going back to church."

She smiled at him and his ribs, the thoughts that had been stressing him out, melted away. Into a deep conviction that Cassie was meant to be in his life. But how? What did God want him to do?

"Daniel? Are your ribs bugging you?" Cassie's query was followed by Amy placing a steeping mug of tea in front of him.

"No, no, I'm good." He looked at Amy. "Thank you.

This is an incredible day for me, and for Cassie. You've done so much for us."

"I understand."

They spent dinner with Bill and his family, sitting at a card table, the type that Cassie associated with the holidays when her parents set them up for the younger kids to sit at, or to put together jigsaw puzzles in the dead of a Pennsylvania winter. It seemed impossible, but between the folding chairs and two stools, they all fit.

They'd both found some closure with Amy's information. She hoped that Amy's grandmother might have more to tell them and looked forward to seeing her later tomorrow in Base Camp.

And yet…she couldn't ignore the empty feeling in the pit of her stomach.

"What do you think about caribou?" Bill ladled more stew into a hollowed-out sourdough bread bowl. They'd devoured two baking sheets' worth of nachos and were finishing up the stew Ramona served her earlier.

"This is delicious, almost as good as my mother's venison stew." She meant it. It might be the fact that she and Daniel hadn't had a solid home-cooked meal in almost a week, and the not-so-small-factor that whenever they ate they'd been worried about wildlife sniffing them out.

"Trevor sure pines for his fast-food burgers while we're up here all summer." Bill ruffled his son's hair, and the entire group busted out laughing, including Trevor.

"Do you take any breaks to go back to Quebec when school's out?" Daniel posed the question to Trevor.

"Naw. The summer up here doesn't last that long. I get two weeks before and after our time here. It's enough. Next year I'll be at university, and I may not get up here as often."

"So you're a senior, Trevor?" Cassie asked.

"Yes, but I'm taking college-level courses this year. Bio."

"That's great. You've certainly been exposed to a wide variety."

"I'm sorry about your great-grandmother, Cassie." Trevor mumbled the words but his sincerity was evident in the brightness in his eyes.

"Awww, thank you. It's okay. More than okay, now that I've been able to leave a family plaque there. Plus say some prayers. It's sad she died so young, doing such a heroic mission, but in many ways I can't think of a more peaceful, beautiful place to pass on. I'll tell my grandmother the same."

"I'm glad you were able to do that. Did you file for the right permits to do so?"

"I did." Cassie was glad she'd crossed all her t's and dotted her i's. Not only from a legal perspective, but as a way to show her respect for all concerned.

"Amy didn't have anything new for you, then?" Ramona stood and began clearing the table. Trevor joined in and motioned for Daniel and Cassie to remain seated. There wasn't enough room for more to do the cleanup, not in the small trailer.

"Thank you for the meal." Cassie handed her plate to Ramona. "Oh, Amy had plenty to share. As a matter of fact, she said her grandmother might have more, and if she does, Amy will meet up with us at Base Camp tomorrow."

Bill shook his head. "It never fails to astound me how much history abounds in this area. If you look at a map, it looks desolate and empty, save for the natural features."

"So true." She thought of Daniel's laminated maps, how they'd provided altitude and topography but didn't display any local villages.

"When I first came here two years ago I was stunned by the constantly changing scenery, how while it's definitely far, this land's been inhabited for eons. And how it looks perfectly normal, like any other regularly traveled northern region. Until the weather happens." Daniel's reverence for history fueled her deep respect for him.

"The weather was most unexpected for me. I read the available tourist information, packed layers, but really had no concept of a snowstorm in August." Cassie smiled at Bill, and then Daniel's gaze caught hers.

Their bond, whether or not either of them wanted to acknowledge it, was tangible. Daniel's brown eyes reflected what she knew was in her heart. So why wasn't she being brave enough to tell him?

Chapter Eighteen

The next morning began early and for once Cassie didn't mind getting back into the cold. Today they'd be safe at Base Camp and ready to start the rest of their lives. The niggling fear of never seeing Daniel again was still there, but she'd turned it over to God in her morning prayers.

"You'll each have your own ATV. I'll drive the one with the extra fuel. We'll probably have to stop up to three times to refuel, depending. Here's yours, Cassie. Have your ridden one before?"

"Only once or twice." With friends, in hills populated by deer and fox, with the occasional black bear. "What do we do if we see a moose?"

"Go around it." Bill grinned then set out to demonstrate all the different gears. "It's not complicated. The gear mitts are more for comfort now, it's not cold enough to need them."

"Okay." She eyed the ATV Daniel had been assigned. It was larger and had a wider base than hers.

"Don't worry about having the smaller one. I gave

Daniel our most stable model, to keep his ribs happier. Yours will manage the trickier parts more easily."

"Define *tricky*." Daniel's concern for her hadn't lessened. She'd felt his gaze on her last night and was determined to demonstrate to him that she was fine without him. He could worry about himself now. While she worked on ignoring the pangs of sadness that licked against her stomach each time she imagined the last time she'd see him. Probably at Base Camp before she boarded the first of many planes back to PA. If Daniel got the go-ahead from the base camp doctor, he planned to stay, to come back out here and make a more formal survey of the B-17. Now that he didn't have her to worry about, why shouldn't he? She didn't need an escort back to Hershey.

Letting go of her protector was hard.

But the most difficult thing to process, to accept, was that both she and Daniel had serious trust issues when it came to relationships. He'd been hurt by his ex-fiancée, and she'd had her heart broken in the past. They were each independent, fully capable of living on their own. Yet wouldn't it be nice if they took a chance on leaning on each other?

"There will be some steep crevasses we need to go into and back up out of as circumnavigating them would mean hundreds of miles in either direction. Cassie's vehicle will be like a sprite, whereas both of ours might take some finessing. Right now we'll each have our own ATV, but we've got to be flexible. If we come upon any rough spots, I'll use Cassie's ATV to ferry me back and forth to bring the other ATVs across. If we need to pair up on the ATVs, we'll do that. Whatever it takes."

"Okay." Daniel's less than enthusiastic agreement stoked her ire. While Bill tanked up the empty fuel canisters next to the garage, she took advantage of her opening and walked over to Daniel, who was busy strapping his pack to the small cargo trailer attached to his ATV.

"I'm not incapable of doing this, Daniel."

"Who said you were?" He looked up at her, his eyes guarded with defensiveness. "We need to be focused on getting out of here, Cassie." He turned back to his gear.

"My pack's stowed, and I need to talk to you before we're done. I don't want you worrying about me on the way to Base Camp. We've made it this far, and you've done so much for me, for my family. I can't ever repay you, but I can give you freedom from thinking you're responsible for me. Bill's with us, we're on motorized vehicles, and only hours from being finished. I mean, I'll be finished."

"You already booked your flight back." His voice was flat, without emotion. But the sparks in his eyes, the way his jaw looked as tight as a mousetrap about to spring, told a different story.

"You're angry at me for that?" She'd used the Wi-Fi connection at Bill and Ramona's and confirmed a seat back to Nain and then Goose Bay. She was on standby for the trip to Toronto and then Harrisburg, where it was a short drive to Hershey. "You said you were stay-ing if you could. I can go back and call now, book you a flight."

"No, that's not what I want." He stopped, and stared at the horizon, conflict etched in the grim line of his mouth. Only after he drew in a few breaths, visibly exhaled, did he face her again. "We've formed a unique bond that's not uncommon for people who've survived what we have. I'm being overprotective, and I know it. Plus, I hate being called out with my own words, is all."

"You think what we've shared is only because of the circumstances?" Hurt pierced her defenses. No matter how he answered, she knew her truth. Daniel had been a gift to her, and if only for a week, she'd accept it. Few people got to enjoy such soul intimacy ever during their time on earth.

"Well, yeah. It's kind of—" He stopped at Bill's wave.

"Time to go, folks. The sun doesn't wait for us to be ready." Bill spoke next to them and Cassie all but jumped. And there it was. How she was so totally engrossed in her conversation with Daniel, how she'd not heard Bill's approach, how she'd missed the gentle dawn breaking in spectacular streaks of crimson as they'd prepared to depart. A soft glow of bluish white had clung to the horizon past midnight, awaiting the earth's turn to full daylight. All underscored what her heart already knew but couldn't share. Not with Daniel. Not now. He may have sacrificed his best days to unearth and catalogue what was left of Eugenia's B-17, all because he thought he had to get her back to Base Camp, out of the wilderness.

"Sure thing." She watched Bill turn back toward the ATV with the fuel and looked at Daniel. "What were you going to say?"

"Nothing, Cassie. It's time to go. Bill's right. No time to waste."

Cassie fought around the lump in her throat, wanting to speak up, tell Daniel exactly how she felt. But sometimes timing was indeed everything. Maybe she'd been spared from making a total fool of herself and laying unnecessary guilt on Daniel. It wasn't his fault that she'd fallen for him, hard.

Please, God. Show me Your will.

It was the only prayer she knew to be true, and always necessary.

Sun reflected off the undulating ground and it was as if diamonds had been scattered across it. The constant twinkling was a gentle reminder that no matter how her brain tried to compare the scenery to the familiar, it couldn't. There was nothing that resembled the way what looked like a flat plain would unexpectedly reveal itself to be a high one, with huge channels that had to be crossed. The water was fairly shallow in many parts and she didn't want to imagine what it'd be like crossing the streams and gullies in the height of spring melt. She'd wanted to view several glaciers as promised by the tour website but figured she'd probably landed in a glacier lake a week ago. That was enough for her. As was what she'd found out about Eugenia. She kept telling herself that it wouldn't matter if Amy didn't turn up or showed up with nothing new about the B-17.

What she already knew had to be enough for now.

What Cassie hadn't expected was how alone and solitary of a trip it was atop an ATV, wearing a helmet, holding on to the handlebars for hours on end. The vibration of the engine and ground that swept beneath her was bone jarring and she knew it couldn't be very easy for Daniel.

There was no way of telling as he rode ahead of her, guided by Bill's voice that sounded in all their helmets. With Bill driving the fuel supply behind her, Cassie was in the middle, "because you're on the quickest and we don't want to lose you," according to Bill.

She thought her stomach was rumbling but couldn't be sure, not with the noise and vibrations. Her fuel gauge was below a quarter of a tank and they'd been driving for at least three hours, which made it four or five since breakfast. Which had been so much earlier than she was used to.

"Let's stop here. Daniel, stop your vehicle and Cassie, you pull up next to him. Nice and easy." Cassie did as he said and shut off her engine. Only once she was next to Daniel with Bill on the other side did she take off her helmet and look out in front of them. More woods, and lots of trees.

"I had no idea we were still so high up." She'd thought their stay at the outpost camp had been at ground level, since they'd hiked partway along the fjord.

"It was all formed by glaciers, as you probably know." Bill unpacked their lunch from one of his containers and she had to strain to hear him. Her ears hummed as if she'd been to a concert at the Hersheypark stadium. The memory of attending a Christian music festival with Jim flashed and she had to bite her lip to keep from giggling. She was so not that woman anymore! Cassie wasn't sure yet that she was ready for a forever commitment, but if she was, Daniel was the only man she'd consider it with. To think she'd tried to put Jim, and other men, into her future seemed juvenile, after what she and Daniel had experienced.

"What's tickling your funny bone?" Daniel never missed her amusement and it warmed her to know he was still paying attention, if somewhat reluctantly.

"I'm thinking about who I thought I was only a year ago. So much has changed, but mostly in the last week. I never believed a single trip could affect me so much."

"Believe it. There's nothing like being out in the middle of literally nowhere, and yet being aware that it's the center of the universe for all the creatures and relatively few humans who live here."

"That's all you think it is, Daniel?"

His breath hitched. "No, Cassie. I know I've changed in ways I've yet to appreciate."

"That's a deep thought." Bill handed them each a brown bag, pointed at the food storage chest. "Help yourselves to water as your bottles get empty."

Cassie bit into Ramona's caribou sandwich and groaned with delight. "This hits the spot."

As they ate, Bill and Daniel spoke about the chances of Daniel coming back with Bill, how they'd tow one of the ATVs or lend it out to someone at Base Camp, which was full of researchers, often in need of extra equipment. Cassie's mind drifted from the reality of parting ways with Daniel back to the myriad feelings she'd been sorting through since yesterday. The need to tell him how she felt, even if it made her vulnerable to the probable rejection as Daniel had continually stressed he wasn't looking for love, resurfaced.

"Okay, time to saddle back up. The most dangerous stretch is ahead of us."

"Dangerous? Do you mean there are more water crossings?"

Bill shook his head. "No. Yes, there are several more dips, trust me, but we're also going to see more wildlife. It's time for them to fatten up, before winter sets in."

Bill flashed a grin. "If we see bear, though, let's take it easy. Usually they ignore these loud machines, but I've had them come out of nowhere before. Always managed to outmaneuver them, but a fired-up bear can keep pace with an ATV for more than I care to admit. We'd outlast it, but I don't want to take any chances."

"Maybe you should take the lead. I can follow Cassie."

"I was just going to suggest that. It won't be so straightforward as we get into the thick of the forests. But, on the positive side, we've only got another two hours to go."

Two hours, and they had to remain alert and ready to respond at a second's notice. Cassie walked to her ATV and closed her eyes, sent up a prayer. They'd made it this far, so what was she so afraid of? Where was her faith?

Daniel appreciated that Bill gave him the more stable ATV, especially as the ground offered plenty of jaw-clenching bumps that sent bolts of pain through his rib cage. He couldn't imagine what it would have been like on Cassie's vehicle.

It had taken every ounce of self-control, and a lot of extra prayers on the way, for him to stay focused on the rugged path in front of them and not keep checking his side-view mirrors for Cassie. Whenever he did check, she was tucked so in line with him that he barely made her out. Bill trailed behind, to either side, as they'd planned. It let him know that not only was Bill safe, but Cassie, as well.

Cassie hadn't spoken a whole lot on the journey this morning. He ached to ask her what was on her mind, her heart. But he hadn't earned the right to. It was for the best, her best, to not make promises he couldn't keep. And what kind of promises did he think he wanted to commit to? Other than his one attempt at being engaged, he'd been careful to never make romantic promises he couldn't keep. It had been for the women he'd met as much as himself.

But Cassie—Cassie wasn't another person he'd simply dated and left it at friends. They'd fast-forwarded through all the usual norms of getting to know each other; they'd had to. If the trust they'd developed between them hadn't happened, he doubted they'd be safely navigating their way to Base Camp but possibly would have shared Sean's tragic fate. He knew she trusted him with her life; she'd proved it time and again. And he completely trusted her. Cassie was as solid a wilderness partner as anyone he'd ever hiked with. If she didn't know something, she was quick to admit it, and he hoped he proved that he offered her the same respect and trust.

You never told her.

Had he really never told her how much he trusted her?

His wheels bumped over a ground swell and reverberated through his skeleton, making his ribs sing to him again. He knew Gus was right; he'd busted a couple, for sure. Between the fractured ribs and probable kidney infection—which was already feeling better, thanks to the horse-sized antibiotic pills Gus gave him—he knew he'd never take his health for granted again. His father often spoke of how getting older made a man respect life and all its blessings that much more. He might only be in his early thirties but he found himself completely agreeing with Dad. And while he'd never planned on it, he'd felt closer to God this trip than at any other time.

It wasn't due to the life-threatening circumstances, either. Watching how Cassie relied so completely on God and her faith, saying those silent prayers with her head bowed, or reaching for his hand to pray together, had changed him. God was no longer only his Creator to talk to about cursory life events, or to reach for during a crisis.

God was his best friend, his everything. And he had no doubt God had put Cassie in his life. The question was, what was he going to do with this precious present? He'd meant it when he told Cassie he wanted to find a church home. But now all he could picture was attending service…with her. Living the Christian life with every fiber of his being, alongside the woman he knew was for him.

There was no way of knowing if his feelings, or Cassie's, were reactions or the real deal. One thing this trip had indelibly etched into his heart—he needed to pray whenever he had any doubt.

Father, show me the way to go. You know what I want, what I think I need. May Your will be done.

They drove along and Daniel was able to make peace with his thoughts, for now. He'd start looking into finding a church home as soon as he was back in Pennsylvania. That would be a good start.

"Let's slow the pace, folks. Bear to your right." Bill's voice had Daniel looking over his shoulder at the hills that rolled up and out to the right, the south, as they headed east toward Base Camp. And the two unmistakable white shapes that contrasted against the moss green ground. Polar bears.

"Cassie, no! Turn. Back. Repeat. Turn. Back." Bill's cry stunned him and he looked for Cassie, but she'd gone off track, way to the right of the course they followed. He watched with horror as she made a direct line for the exact place where the mother bear and cub stood. The momma bear had switched from a detached, observational stance to full-on defensive, her massive head hanging between the unfathomable strength of her shoulders, placing herself between her cub and Cassie.

As if she only now heard Bill's directive, and saw the bears, Cassie swung wildly to the left. For a suspended moment in time, her vehicle reared onto two side wheels, still moving forward, no longer toward but not far enough away from, the bears.

Slow down. Slow down. Please, God.

He acted on instinct, heading directly for the bears, knowing he had to give them a distraction from Cassie. She was too close, and while the ATVs could ultimately outrun a polar bear, theoretically, Daniel didn't want to see it proven. His mind raced with bear statistics. Grown female, weight one thousand pounds, height seven feet, speed twenty-five miles per hour when sprinting. And what better motivation to sprint than believing your cub was under attack?

Sure enough, even as his ATV covered the uneven ground at the steep angle, the bear paid no mind as she began to chase after Cassie. Daniel's entire consciousness seemed to separate from his body as he headed straight toward the animal.

"Daniel, no! Slow down and turn back. I'll get the bear. Cassie, keep—" Bill's words halted as they both saw what they feared most. Cassie's ATV was on its side, unable to maintain the two-wheeled side motion. It flipped down the hill, as if no more than a tiny metal toy car. He didn't care about the ATV as his gaze hungrily searched for a sign of Cassie. Her still, lifeless form on the side of the hill seared into his brain and heart as his lungs fought for air, unable to breathe in more than short, panicked gasps.

He stopped his ATV next to her, got off, and rushed to her side. Her pale face, closed eyes behind the helmet's visor triggered the most primal sense of powerlessness he'd ever felt as his chest constricted further and his hands clenched. On his knees, his arms ached to reach to the sky, howl at the intense pain ricocheting through his heart.

No, God, no. Not Cassie.

Chapter Nineteen

Cassie's head *thunked* against the ground, no matter that she was clenching her core as tight as possible as she landed. Being airborne for a few seconds had given her time to think, for her body to react to the accident.

She opened her eyes to the blue sky above, and a dark figure looming over her. The polar bear?

Daniel.

He was gently lifting her visor, and she swore she felt the tension in his every move. When his gaze finally met hers, she tried to smile, to speak.

"I—" No more came out of her mouth as speaking required the breath that had been knocked out of her.

"Don't move, not yet. Can you feel this?" He gripped one of her hands, then the other.

"Yeah." A bare whisper when she wanted to shout that they needed to get out of here. She tried to sit up.

"Whoa, wait."

Cassie didn't have time for this. "I'm fine. It was a rough tumble is all. But—" Her words came easier, though she suspected her shoulders, back and noggin were going to bother her later. As her gaze went past his shoulder, to where she'd mistakenly gone, she froze in place, still seated on the ground as she watched. The bears. Bill was circling the mother bear, at a distance, and had somehow distracted her from Cassie and Daniel. But she didn't think the bear had forgotten them. "We have to help Bill."

Daniel shot a quick glance over his shoulder before turning back to her. "Can you still ride?"

"I—I think so." With his help, she clambered up to her feet. But as they approached her overturned ATV, she saw the puddle of liquid on the otherwise dry ground. And smelled it. Fuel. Gasoline.

"You won't be going on this vehicle." Daniel's grim pronouncement made her wince. No way would she travel with him, as he couldn't handle the pain of someone holding his ribs. Which left Bill, who was acting as a polar matador, except trying to get the bear away from them.

"He can't keep doing that." She spoke to Daniel as he put his helmet back on, to talk to Bill, she assumed. Cassie did the same.

"Bill, Cassie's safe but her ATV's fuel tank is punctured."

"Get on your ATV together and keep heading away. I'll meet you farther along the trek." Bill's voice was remarkably calm as he worked at saving all of their lives.

"Copy." Daniel looked at her and pointed to his ATV. "Let's go."

She walked in front as he indicated, the ground rough and uneven under her hiking boots. Unprotected by the large wheels, she was acutely aware of the terrain they'd traversed and how difficult if not impossible it might have been for her and Daniel to make it to Base Camp on their own. Bill had saved their lives and continued to.

Daniel swung his leg over and sat down, and she followed suit.

"Hang on."

"I'm good." She hung on to the rear quad bar—the same piece of equipment that had saved her from being crushed when her ATV flipped—unwilling to risk hurting his ribs further. He revved the engine and they took off.

It seemed simple. Daniel had to get them to a point far enough along their trajectory for Bill to meet them while leaving the bears behind. She figured Bill was betting on the mother bear not running too far from her cub, no matter how much it looked like she'd chased them the entire way into Base Camp. She watched Bill's skillful maneuvering and used the time to pray for all of them. She'd have included Daniel, said the prayer aloud, but didn't want to risk distracting either him or Bill. They could have a prayer of thanksgiving together after they reached Base Camp.

Thank You for keeping us safe. Please protect Bill. Bless Daniel—

The ATV hit something and they were flying through the air, as if they'd gone up a ramp in a stunt. Her arms tensed as her mind told them to reach for Daniel. But she couldn't convince her hands to loosen their grip on the quad bar, behind her at the arch of her back. She looked all around for a point of reference and only saw a wide, gaping chasm beneath them. They were flying across a small gully, one they no doubt were supposed to traverse by trekking down to the stream she saw pass under the ATV, then back up. She didn't see how they'd reach the other side, not from her vantage point.

All the thoughts raced through her mind as time stood still, and she realized her and Daniel's lives were in the balance.

She closed her eyes, tried to pray. The ATV hit the ground with jarring force, and her fingers were ripped from the quad bar as she was flung from the seat. A sickening *crack* of her helmet that reverberated through her skull, her jaws, and Cassie's world went dark once again.

Daniel stopped the ATV, stunned that they'd cleared the gully. He turned to make sure Cassie was doing okay, only to find the seat empty. Because she'd been holding on to the rear quad bar he didn't know she was gone. What if she was in the gully? Had she fallen while still in range of the bear, on the other side of the small stream?

On the ground, he quickly surveyed the area. Bill's ATV roared in the background, and he had to trust the man was safe and getting away from the bear. He had to find Cassie.

He turned to the right to begin his scan and his heart burst open at the same instant his stomach twisted in a painful, physical reaction to seeing her lying motionless for the second time today.

Please, please, please.

He knew God heard him, that he didn't need to be formal. All he prayed for was in those three words.

But it wasn't a repeat of moments earlier when Cassie

had sprung up as would a gymnast from a pit of foam blocks. Her leg was twisted at an unnatural angle, her head to the side. He dropped to his knees, repeated what he'd done earlier to check for possible paralysis. But there was no response from Cassie, her eyes firmly closed and her breath shallow against his hand when he checked to make sure he didn't need to do CPR.

He'd had enough first aid and wilderness training to know he couldn't move her, couldn't risk harming her further. They were less than thirty minutes from base, but it may as well have been a day. There was nothing he could do. Helpless and defeated, at the end of his survival skills, he stared at the one woman he'd ever loved.

What would Cassie do?

"Heavenly Father, I beseech You to help Cassie. Please let her live. Show me what to do next. I do not know what Your will is, please, tell me."

The roar of Bill's engine shook him from his prayer and he looked around. No Bill in sight, not yet. But there, only one hundred yards away yet a world apart thanks to the run-off crevice, stood the mother bear. On her hind legs, snout angled. Huge paws that meant a man's death, which could have been Cassie's fate, hanging almost casually. He saw her voluminous underbelly, as well as the quivering of her nostrils. The bear was incapable of jumping the ravine but he didn't underestimate her ability to climb down and up the literal roadblock. It would take her a while, but not long enough.

Seeing her cub in the distance, searching for its mom, he knew what he had to do. He pulled Sean's flare gun from his pocket, where he'd kept it since the crash. In a matter of seconds he fired one, then a second, warning shot toward the cub. The mother fell to her four paws, growling. The sound with zero question of intent raised the hairs on his nape, but he had to know she was going back to her cub. The rifle was still around his back. He didn't want to shoot, but would if he had to.

Please, God.

In what had to be a record for his most quickly answered prayer, the polar bear turned and ran off, toward her offspring. When they met up, they kept going, toward the horizon. Away from where he stood next to Cassie's still form. Granting Daniel the reprieve he needed.

Without hesitation he drew his phone and pressed the speed dial for Base Camp emergency services. And prayed he wasn't too late.

Deep, penetrating cold rushed through her right leg, from her pelvis to her knee. She opened her eyes a crack, saw the ground at an odd angle through her helmet's visor. No, she was the one at the strange position as she lay atop the rocky path they'd been speeding over.

"Yes, that's right. Estimate we're no farther than thirty minutes from base. You do? Fantastic. Please hurry." Daniel's voice washed comfort over her and she couldn't even see him. Where was he?

The ATV. Jumping the crevice. Memories rushed in and triggered a pounding in her skull that made her vision blur. She closed her eyes, breathed in and out.

Please help me. Keep Daniel safe.

"Cassie, it's Daniel. Please don't move if you hear me. I'm going to raise your visor." She waited until the cool Newfoundland-Labrador air washed over her face, helping some of the pain in her head ease off. But not her leg. It was definitely injured but she didn't want to know how badly. She'd survived Daniel's daring yet necessary jump across the two edges of the run-off bed. She was still alive!

"How are you, Cassie?" Daniel's face filled her vision and she was grateful she'd gathered the nerve to open her eyes again. She clung to his gaze, to the promise of a happy ending for what had been the longest week of her life. "You took a bit of a spill again."

"I'm fine." Her voice was stronger than it had been when she'd taken the tumble earlier. "I can wiggle my toes."

"Don't. Move." Clouds of concern raced over his expression, dropping deep worry into the depths of his eyes. She'd never seen such beautiful eyes, such lush lashes. It made her smile.

"What's funny?" His voice, soft and gentle while buoying her with its strength, wrapped around her.

"You. Your lashes are what every girl longs for."

"Ah, okay." Lines between his brows indicated he thought she'd been shaken badly by the fall.

"I'm just…glad. Happy to be alive." The image of a mother polar bear and her cub flashed across her mind. "The bear! Oh no, Daniel—" She tried to force herself on her elbow, but before she could raise more than her head, the searing pain in her leg struck as she reflexively moved it for support. A long, hard wail sounded and it took her a minute or two—or was it an hour?—to realize it was hers. The pain triggered nausea and she shut her eyes again, afraid of throwing up. Cassie hated vomiting as much as she hated heights.

"I've got you, Cassie. The helicopter will be here soon. You're not alone. I'm here, and Bill's standing not far, waving it in for a clean landing."

"Thank you." She wanted to tell him so much more. It was there, the thoughts she'd come up with that had occurred to her, this past day or two. But her mind wasn't cooperating and she couldn't grasp the right words. "Daniel..."

"Don't talk. Rest. I'm so sorry about the pain. About the fall. About all of this. I—" He stopped at the same time she heard, then felt, a huge rumbling across the land. It had to be the life flight.

After all they'd been through, she was going to be flown out at the very last bit of the journey. And she hated it.

"Daniel, listen." She had to tell him, let him know. But he was gone, and she was being addressed by a strange woman. First she was examined, then placed onto a hard board. Somewhere in her brain she recognized that her pain when they moved her leg was a good thing. She hadn't been paralyzed, and a leg could be fixed. But it felt as though the limb was going to fall off. Another medic of some sort rolled back her sleeve and she never felt the prick of the needle she knew had to be on the end of the syringe. Her awareness grew hot, then cold and fuzzy as they lifted her, carried her.

"Daniel." She yelled as loudly as she could, but it sounded like a whisper amid the noise of the rotors, still turning. Terror gripped her. She couldn't do this alone.

"Cassie." He had her hand, running next to the board. "You'll be okay. You've got this."

"No, no. I can't get on this plane." Her words slurred

and she fought to focus on him, his gaze. She needed Daniel's strength now more than ever.

"Hang in there, Cassie!" Daniel's shout was the last thing she heard. For the third time on the same day, Cassie's world went dark.

Chapter Twenty

"Hang in there."

Two hours later, Daniel keenly missed Cassie. Had those really been the last words he'd said to her? Possibly the last thing she'd remember him by? Remorse battered at him as he sat in the plastic chair at the medical clinic. He'd been examined and Gus's diagnosis of a kidney infection validated. Cracked ribs and several large bruises rounded off his mementos from the week with Cassie. All he waited for was a flight back to Pennsylvania. Cassie was probably already en route to a hospital in Quebec, if not all the way to the States depending upon what flights were available. If she was in any shape to travel. If…

Don't go there. She had to live.

Cassie. Would she pay the ultimate price for his actions?

"You're a hard man to track down, Daniel." Amy's voice stabbed through his misery as she walked into his exam room with a concerned look on her face. "I heard you saved some lives today."

"I'm not so sure about that." Cassie had regained consciousness before the life flight arrived, but had been in horrible pain. He feared for internal bleeding, broken bones, but all he could do was watch as the EMTs did the painstaking work of strapping her to a spinal board. She'd cried out when her leg was touched and it was as if it was his own limb.

"Tell me, Amy, what have you heard about Cassie? The staff hasn't told me anything yet."

"They tell me Cassie's been flown to Nain. Probable broken leg. She'll be okay. I know Doc Martin, the ER boss there, and he's the best."

Thank You, God. He nodded, unable to respond any other way. His mind went back to those last words he'd shared with Cassie. The last time he'd looked upon her dear, beloved face.

Cassie had spoken with Bill and him while they'd waited for the helicopter. He'd been astounded, and touched, by her pure sincerity as she'd looked at him, tears of pain leaking from the corners of her eyes. She'd looked at him as if he held the key to everything as she kept talking, despite her agony.

"I'm so sorry, Daniel. I thought Bill said to bear right. Turn right. This is all my fault."

"Oh, Cassie." He'd wanted to call her *dear, babe, sweetheart*, but his right to that was forfeited when he'd not admitted his feelings to himself in time to tell her. She deserved more than being emotionally jerked around by him.

No. First he had to have solo time with himself, with God, to make sure. No more putting Cassie or her heart in danger.

He'd promised her there and then to call as soon as they were both back home. He had to trust God with the rest. That prayer, thought and time would make the answer clear for him.

"Daniel, I brought you something." Amy's voice ripped him from his memory as she sat in the chair next to him.

"I'm sorry, Amy." He couldn't stop the thoughts competing for his attention. If he'd checked on Cassie, made certain that she'd understood Bill's instructions, she'd be sitting here with him and not have needed to be life flighted to Nain.

"No worries, I get it. You've been through a lot." She placed what he thought was a computer bag on her lap and pulled out a worn weathered wooden box. "This is what my grandmother had for all these years. It's what was found with the B-17. The story goes that when it crashed it made a huge fireball, and my great-grandparents couldn't go near it for several days. By the time they got there, the remains of the pilot and two other crew were pretty much all ashes. But they found this." She handed him the box, the size of a cigar box, and he opened it.

Several items of jewelry, including two large wedding bands that he thought were for a man, along with two equally masculine-looking wristwatches. A tiny drawstring bag, stained coffee brown with age, fit neatly in his palm.

"Should I open it?"

Amy nodded.

He untied it and turned the bag upside down. A fine gold chain spilled out onto his open hand, revealing a small gold cross and simple gold wedding band. Eager to confirm it was Eugenia's, he turned both the ring and cross over and around, peering at any marks he could see. The cross didn't have any engraving, but the wedding band told him what he needed when he saw *Eugenia Smith Haas* engraved in cursive. He held what Cassie had come here for.

The personal jewelry items were the treasure, what mattered the most. The symbol of Eugenia's deep faith, shared by her great-granddaughter.

"It's Cassie's great-grandmother's." His heart was a battlefield as joy warred with despair. His head pounded with regret and resignation. This could have been in Cassie's hands already; she would have been able to take it back to Hershey with her.

"She already had the dog tags, as they were sent to her great-grandfather. Your grandparents must have been the ones to see that they got them." He looked at Amy.

"Yes. I imagine they turned them in to the Canadian Armed Forces and told them the remains were either buried or didn't exist. I don't know. From there they were sent to the States. The story I've been told is that my family found the extra treasures several years after the crash, after the war had ended. Grandma says her mother probably meant to find the rightful owner but never got around to it. I'm so glad to be able to give you these other mementos. You'll see Cassie again, right? You said you're both from Pennsylvania." Amy spoke matter-of-factly.

"We live four hours apart."

"You've hiked more ground, Daniel." Amy's grin

was infectious, and he couldn't stop his mouth from curving up if only by a millimeter.

"We have." He nodded. "I can't thank you enough for this. Cassie will be over the moon." How he'd get it to her, when he'd see her again, were questions he needed time to sort through.

"There's more, though."

Curious, he watched her take another box from the bag. "Both the box with the crew members' valuables, and this, were in a sealed metal container and stored in the tail." She handed him a much fancier box, carved with inlaid wood that reminded him of very old European jewelry and keepsake boxes. "I don't know where these are from or to whom they belong, but since you're the first person anyone's taken seriously since 1943, my family and I want to entrust them to you. Find their home, Daniel."

He opened the tiny latch, then the ornate cover. Nestled inside the velvet-lined container were several jeweled brooches and a breathtaking emerald-and-ruby necklace. Exactly what his employer had been searching for.

Both he and Cassie had found what they'd come to the Torngat Mountains for. But was it case closed? Or was there another treasure they'd forsaken?

Three weeks later

The strains of "Happy Birthday" were so loud it seemed the Hershey, Pennsylvania, restaurant venue's roof should lift. Cassie stood, with the aid of crutches, behind Grandma Rose and watched her blow out all eighty-five candles on the luscious lemon cake. Tears pooled at the edges of her lower lids, and she knew everyone would assume they were from the joy of surviving her ordeal, giving Grandma her wish, and being back home. Her real reward had been when Grandma sat next to her on the sofa, absorbing every word Cassie told her about the trip. About her mother. Grandma Rose cried when she saw the photos of where her mother had died and gone on to meet her Creator.

It should have been enough, to see her grandma so happy. But Cassie was in a kind of pain she'd never experienced before. The pain of being apart from the only one for her. God knew her heartache, how much she missed Daniel. She poured out her anguish in prayer morning, noon, and night.

They hadn't seen one another since the Torngat Mountains. It was by mutual agreement. They needed some time to make sure they weren't reacting to what they'd been through. Daniel said they both needed to pray on their futures, and she thought he meant their mutual future. But she hadn't pressed him to meet sooner, or to figure it out right away.

Daniel had faithfully texted or called each day, and they'd even videochatted and said prayers together. But no mention of what they meant to each other, if they were going to take the bond formed under traumatic circumstances any further.

Cassie knew Daniel was the man for her, but he had to figure out if she was right for him. She appreciated Daniel's thoughtfulness in seeing they needed time for God to make things more clear. But she also missed him like all get out.

No matter how much she knew it was for the best, she hoped that they'd come up with a time to talk in person soon. As each day passed, though, she wondered if Daniel had changed his mind. He'd never committed to anything, nor had he told her he loved her.

She hadn't told him her heart's truth, either. Or anyone in her family. She'd only taken her deepest feelings for Daniel to God in her prayer time.

"Here we go." Grandma smiled as she cut into the cake, and Cassie put her crutches to the side to help hand it out. Her leg was broken but she was perfectly able to stand on her good one while helping.

"Sit down." She ignored her mother's whisper and kept handing out the cake, one slice after another to the thirty-odd people gathered around.

"Thank you." A deep, familiar, much-missed voice. Cassie stared at the hand that accepted the plate, unable to trust herself to verify her deepest wish. "Cassie."

She looked up, past the navy blue suit, pale blue dress shirt and yellow tie, and into the gaze she'd fallen into the minute she'd met him.

"Daniel." She blinked. "I've never seen you so, so—"

"Dressed?" The flash of his grin gave her the strength to gather her wits.

"Yes." She looked around at her family, their close friends. "Everyone, this is Daniel Sturges. The man responsible for saving my life."

Cassie expected everyone to introduce themselves, as her family was by no means a shy lot. So she was puzzled by their silence. She sought out her mother.

"Mom?"

"We know Daniel, honey. We've already met." Her father spoke up and she caught the wink he threw Daniel.

"Okay? What's going on, then?" She slowly put the cake knife down, not caring about smooshing frosting onto the pale pink tablecloth. Grandma Rose immediately swiped a dollop of the frosting with her finger and plopped it in her mouth.

"Delicious. Hurry up, Daniel, so that we can get on with the party!" Grandma Rose's eyes, the same shade as Cassie's, sparked with knowing.

With love.

"Here, honey, have a seat." Her mother moved a chair so that everyone gathered could see her and Daniel. Daniel helped her lower onto the cushion, and propped her broken leg on an overturned box. Her crutches were out of reach, so there was no escaping whatever came next.

Daniel took the chair next to her. His gaze was enigmatic as he took her hands.

"I'm sorry I didn't call or come see you sooner. But I had to get a few things in order first." He spoke in low tones, just for her. "In a few minutes, I'm going to give your grandmother proof that the treasure from Eugenia's flight has been returned to the rightful owners, the church where they were taken from, for safekeeping."

"That's wonderful! But wait. Did you get your bonus?"

"I got the bonus I was supposed to get, Cassie. My employer has already arranged for the transfer of the jewelry to the Hermitage in Saint Petersburg, Russia. And I've given my bonus to Way Point, to build an education center with new computer and internet equipment. But those are material matters." She soaked in his presence, her heart thumping as joy began to unfurl in her core.

"That's wonderful, Daniel! I'm sorry you didn't make more money for your cause." After all they'd been through, all he'd fought for with this trip, and what the nature education center meant to him.

"There's absolutely nothing to be sorry for, Cassie. I got my reward." He drew her close, his hands took hers.

"You did?"

He nodded, their eyes locked, and her heart beat with what she saw reflected in his eyes. "I grew closer to God, and my faith is stronger than ever. All because of you, Cassie."

"I love you, Daniel."

"I love you, Cassie."

They spoke in unison, which drew a joyous collective gasp from the crowd. Both Cassie and Daniel laughed before she then lifted her face and closed her eyes. The kiss held the promise of a lifetime of love.

"It's been awful without you, Daniel. Why haven't you called, or come sooner?"

"I wanted to give you space and time, Cassie. I needed it, too. To discern the truth. Our attachment isn't the by-product of a traumatic experience."

He reached into his jacket pocket and withdrew a jewelry box. "I have two gifts, one for you and one for Grandma Rose." He handed Grandma Rose the box, which she opened immediately. And gasped.

"It's lovely!" She lifted up a gold chain, with a small gold cross. "Was it…"

Daniel nodded. "It was your mother's." Cassie's

breath caught at the expression of awe on Grandma Rose's face. Her family may have been working with Daniel to surprise her, but he hadn't told them everything. Her mother's cheeks were wet and her father was beaming.

"My father gave it to her for their first anniversary, right as the war started. He told me about it." Grandma Rose's eyes shone and she held the necklace up to her daughter with shaking fingers. "Here, put it on me, please."

Daniel turned back to Cassie. "Are you ready for your surprise?" He squeezed her hands and she nodded.

"I can't wait." Her insides were quaking and her face was hot with anticipation. When Daniel got to one knee and took out a second small jewelry box, she was grateful her mother had sat her down, awkward leg in a mobile cast or not.

"Cassie Edmunds, we've endured the oddest and most impractical, practical, getting-to-know-you time ever. We both were on a journey to find treasure. And I found the most valuable treasure of all. My heart. I love you, I am in love with you and I need you at my side. Will you do me the honor of agreeing to be at my side from now until forever?"

Cassie stared at him and had never been so certain in her life. "I love you, too. Yes, Daniel. Yes!" The crowd applauded as he lifted her from the chair and pulled her into his arms. Their kiss was warm, delicious and full of promise. Cassie didn't care what it was going to take, this was the man she knew God had sent her.

"Wait, Cassie. Here." His face was flush with emotion as he held up the small box and she hugged him tight. It didn't matter what was in the box—she had Daniel.

He popped open the box and she saw two rings. One with a modest diamond, and a plain gold band.

"This is your engagement ring." He placed it on her left ring finger. "The wedding band was Eugenia's. Grandma Rose asked that I give it to you. For when we're married."

Both rings shimmered through her joyous tears. She looked up at him, needing to tell him all that she'd held in for too long.

"I love you, Daniel. I'm willing to consider moving to Pittsburgh." She couldn't keep her thoughts to herself any longer.

He grinned, pulled her closer. "Not necessary. It'd be harder for you to start over, finding a new client base for your counseling practice. And your organizational business. We'll start here, in Harrisburg. You're so close to your family, and I am, too, but I can be back in Pittsburgh often enough. They're all so happy for us and can't wait to meet you. There's an opening for a high school history teacher in your district. I still have a few interviews to go, but it looks good."

"And if it doesn't work out?" She never wanted him to regret giving up so much for her, for them.

"It doesn't matter. All that matters is that we work out, because this is clearly God's will for us. To be together."

"Oh, Daniel." She leaned in for another kiss. "We are so blessed."

* * * * *

Dear Reader,

Welcome to Newfoundland and Labrador, Canada! Not only is it one of the most breathtaking places on God's earth, it's a perfect backdrop for Cassie and Daniel, two headstrong believers, to fall in love. What I enjoyed most about their journey is that while they both have faith, neither is doing what they want to do but have been procrastinating on: going back to church services. It takes their belief in God, and then one another, for them to realize that a believing community is what they've been missing in their lives. As well as each other!

While I've experienced more than a few scary situations when I was on active duty in the navy, I've never been stranded in the mountains. Any mistakes regarding wilderness survival or physical descriptions of the Newfoundland-Labrador region are solely my own.

My deepest wish is that your own faith is strengthened as you read this story of how Cassie and Daniel made theirs stronger. I'm always happy to connect—please find me at my website where you can sign up for my newsletter. I'm also on Instagram and Facebook. All links below.

Peace,
Geri

gerikrotow.com
facebook.com/gerikrotow
instagram.com/geri_krotow

LOVE INSPIRED

Stories to uplift and inspire

Fall in love with Love Inspired—
inspirational and uplifting stories of faith
and hope. Find strength and comfort in
the bonds of friendship and community.
Revel in the warmth of possibility and the
promise of new beginnings.

Sign up for the Love Inspired newsletter
at **LoveInspired.com** to be the first
to find out about upcoming titles,
special promotions and exclusive content.

CONNECT WITH US AT:

f Facebook.com/LoveInspiredBooks

🐦 Twitter.com/LoveInspiredBks

LISOCIAL2021

Get 4 FREE REWARDS!

We'll send you 2 FREE Books plus <u>2</u> FREE Mystery Gifts.

FREE Value Over **$20**

Both the **Love Inspired®** and **Love Inspired® Suspense** series feature compelling novels filled with inspirational romance, faith, forgiveness, and hope.

YES! Please send me 2 FREE novels from the Love Inspired or Love Inspired Suspense series and my 2 FREE gifts (gifts are worth about $10 retail). After receiving them, if I don't wish to receive any more books, I can return the shipping statement marked "cancel." If I don't cancel, I will receive 6 brand-new Love Inspired Larger-Print books or Love Inspired Suspense Larger-Print books every month and be billed just $5.99 each in the U.S. or $6.24 each in Canada. That is a savings of at least 17% off the cover price. It's quite a bargain! Shipping and handling is just 50¢ per book in the U.S. and $1.25 per book in Canada.* I understand that accepting the 2 free books and gifts places me under no obligation to buy anything. I can always return a shipment and cancel at any time. The free books and gifts are mine to keep no matter what I decide.

Choose one: ☐ **Love Inspired Larger-Print** (122/322 IDN GNWC) ☐ **Love Inspired Suspense Larger-Print** (107/307 IDN GNWN)

Name (please print)

Address   Apt. #

City   State/Province   Zip/Postal Code

Email: Please check this box ☐ if you would like to receive newsletters and promotional emails from Harlequin Enterprises ULC and its affiliates. You can unsubscribe anytime.

> **Mail to the Harlequin Reader Service:**
> **IN U.S.A.:** P.O. Box 1341, Buffalo, NY 14240-8531
> **IN CANADA:** P.O. Box 603, Fort Erie, Ontario L2A 5X3

Want to try 2 free books from another series? Call 1-800-873-8635 or visit www.ReaderService.com.

*Terms and prices subject to change without notice. Prices do not include sales taxes, which will be charged (if applicable) based on your state or country of residence. Canadian residents will be charged applicable taxes. Offer not valid in Quebec. This offer is limited to one order per household. Books received may not be as shown. Not valid for current subscribers to the Love Inspired or Love Inspired Suspense series. All orders subject to approval. Credit or debit balances in a customer's account(s) may be offset by any other outstanding balance owed by or to the customer. Please allow 4 to 6 weeks for delivery. Offer available while quantities last.

Your Privacy—Your information is being collected by Harlequin Enterprises ULC, operating as Harlequin Reader Service. For a complete summary of the information we collect, how we use this information and to whom it is disclosed, please visit our privacy notice located at corporate.harlequin.com/privacy-notice. From time to time we may also exchange your personal information with reputable third parties. If you wish to opt out of this sharing of your personal information, please visit readerservice.com/consumerchoice or call 1-800-873-8635. **Notice to California Residents**—Under California law, you have specific rights to control and access your data. For more information on these rights and how to exercise them, visit corporate.harlequin.com/california-privacy.

LIRLIS22

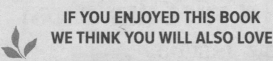

SPECIAL EXCERPT FROM

LOVE INSPIRED SUSPENSE
INSPIRATIONAL ROMANCE

*Framed for murder and corporate espionage,
Haley Whitcombe flees in her plane with evidence
that could clear her name—and is shot out of the sky.
Now trapped in North Cascades National Park,
she must work with park ranger Ezra Dalton to
survive the wilderness and assassins.*

Read on for a sneak preview of
Hunted in the Wilderness *by Kellie VanHorn,
available July 2022 from Love Inspired Suspense!*

"What about the plane?" Haley's voice squeaked like a mouse, and she clapped her mouth shut. *No one* ever saw her this scared or vulnerable.

"If we don't get out of this icy tomb, the plane won't matter." Ezra swiveled away from the safety of the wall to push her closer, then loosened the rope around his arm to lace his fingers together near her foot. "Here."

She stepped onto his interlaced hands and scrabbled up onto the frozen edge of the crevasse. Then he hauled himself up. Rain ran in cold rivulets down her face, soaking her hair, and she swiped at her cheeks as she scanned the sky.

Despite how reckless it was flying in this weather, the plane was still up there. She pointed at the dark shape now swinging around, ready to make another pass.

"They're coming back!" she screamed over the wind.

"Keep going. If we reach the rocks, we'll be harder to see."

Between her black jacket and his brightly colored gear, they were sitting ducks out on the snow. The rocks would be better than nothing.

But as they neared the edge of the ice, the plane shifted course, veering slightly east to where the sky wasn't as dark.

Taking her hand, Ezra helped her down the icy edge of the glacier onto the water-slicked, loose rock at the base of the ridge. Haley stared at the plane as it slowly circled over the area just northeast of them, ascending in altitude with each turn.

"What's that pilot doing?" Ezra yelled over the whipping wind.

"I don't kn—" She broke off, her mouth falling open, as a dark figure climbed out onto the wing and launched into the open air. Then another, and another. Five in total. Her chest tightened, her worst fears confirmed as parachutes exploded from their backs after the jumpers had cleared the plane.

Coming for *her*.

Don't miss
Hunted in the Wilderness *by Kellie VanHorn,*
available July 2022 wherever
Love Inspired Suspense books and ebooks are sold.

LoveInspired.com

IF YOU ENJOYED THIS BOOK, DON'T MISS NEW EXTENDED-LENGTH NOVELS FROM LOVE INSPIRED!

In addition to the Love Inspired books you know and love, we're excited to introduce even more uplifting stories in a longer format, with more inspiring fresh starts and page-turning thrills!

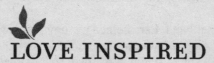

LOVE INSPIRED

Stories to uplift and inspire.

Fall in love with Love Inspired—inspirational and uplifting stories of faith and hope. Find strength and comfort in the bonds of friendship and community. Revel in the warmth of possibility, and the promise of new beginnings.

LOOK FOR THESE LOVE INSPIRED TITLES ONLINE AND IN THE BOOK DEPARTMENT OF YOUR FAVORITE RETAILER!